AF492705

Stepping Stones for Your Spirit

Tales of Turning Points, Hope and Healing

STEPPING STONES

FOR YOUR SPIRIT

TALES OF TURNING POINTS, HOPE AND HEALING

KAREN DAVID

ILLUSTRATED BY
JANE SIBLEY-HAGER

Stepping Stones for Your Spirit
(Tales of Turning Points, Hope and Healing)
Karen David/Mystic Farms
P.O. Box 39216
Cleveland, Ohio 44139
www.kdmystic.net

ISBN: 979-8-218-21359-6
ISBN (e-book): 979-8-218-31139-1

Cover and Interior layout by Victoria Wolf, wolfdesignandmarketing.com,
copyright owned by Karen David.

Illustrations by Jane Sibley-Hager

CONTENTS

Introduction

I CAN'T EXPLAIN how this book came into being. I wasn't thinking about it—it wasn't planned. Yet one day, my mind was filled with an image of power and peacefulness—a lion and a lamb were lying down together. Although this is a familiar spiritual scene, this time I sensed something more was to come.

For years I have journeyed with faith along a road less traveled. Many would call my journey "unconventional." I have had many unusual, unexplained, and mystical experiences. I have also explored a variety of religious and spiritual practices that others have shared with me.

In the process, I have also gained wisdom about how to use—and trust—my own unique intuition. This led me step by step into my own deeply personal relationship with our Lord and Creator.

Spiritual understanding, faith, hope, and most of all love, are essential to bringing wholeness to our being. We all have a spiritual consciousness, as well as a physical consciousness. We are *not* our bodies—we are souls *with* bodies.

Now, back to the image of the lion and the lamb! After it appeared to me in my mind, I received a deep, intuitive impression: "Sit down and write!" It was as if an inner voice was speaking to me. I quietly asked, "Write what? I don't know what to say about this image."

The inner voice message came back, "Just sit down and begin."

The next thing I knew, I was sitting at my computer looking at a blank page. Then, without hesitation, I began writing down every image, thought and scene that entered my mind. Suddenly, a character emerged, then another—and each had something important to learn, experience, and share with you, the reader.

When I write, I don't always have an easy time of it. However, this time the words were flying onto the page. There were actual moments when I couldn't type fast enough to keep up with the ideas that were entering my mind. I had to type quickly to be sure everything was written the way it was intended to appear on the page, and I didn't want to miss a thing.

The first story that came into my mind is titled, "Lion and the Lamb," and features a woman named Casey. After she undergoes a very powerful experience, she chooses to share her message with everyone who reads her story.

Once Casey's story came through, I thought I was finished. But more stories kept coming. I soon realized that this was meant to be a collection—and later, a book.

In closing, the characters in each story such as —Paul and Al in "An Angel Dressed in Cowboy Boots," Sarah in "A Street Lamp and the Perfect Stranger," Joshua in "A Fork in the Road"—are waiting eagerly for you to join them. They want to share what happened to them and how they grew in wisdom as a result.

Writing this book has certainly elevated the joy within my spirit. I'm sharing it with you in hopes it will do the same for you.

Warm wishes, Karen David

A Fork in
the Road

JOSHUA STOOD AT THE FORK of the country road. It was a familiar spot which was about a mile down from his dairy farm. He had taken a leisurely walk and suddenly stopped, remembering he forgot to have that extra key made for the hay room door.

"Are you thinking about something?" a voice asked him.

Joshua spun around quickly, and then raised his hand to shield his eyes from the intense brilliance glowing in front of him.

"Who are you?" Joshua cried out, frightened. He was a husky elderly man at the age of eighty, but still fit and sturdy after years of working on his farm. Joshua's face bore the weathered lines of a man who had been active all his life. Yet, there was an ageless quality about him. Unless someone really knew him, no one at first meeting him would ever have guessed his real age.

The brilliance began to mellow. "Do not be afraid. I have been sent from Heaven, Joshua," came the message, simple yet powerful. The voice was gentle, the tone low-pitched and soothing.

He wasn't sure yet, but Joshua thought he had heard that voice before. He just couldn't put a finger on exactly where.

He felt his knees grow weak, yet he dared to look upon this glowing light again, and now saw the image of a slender, youthful looking male dressed in a simple one-piece garment.

"Do not be afraid," came the sound of the voice through the radiant light.

In all his faith-filled years, Joshua could not even fathom that an angel would ever appear before him, and he felt himself on the verge of passing out from the encounter.

The angelic spirit quickly caught his arm and helped him from falling. "Steady there, friend," soothed the being, his luminous smile and calm, refreshing tone were warm and comforting.

"You are a faithful and pious man, Joshua Kale," the angel said having helped him regain his balance. "You've chosen to live simply and with whatever the Lord brought into your life. You always accepted what happened to you as His Will. God has allowed that you receive the gift of knowing that angels do, indeed, exist. I am your guardian angel."

"My guardian angel!" Joshua stood there, barely able to breathe. Throughout this encounter, he felt as if he were basking in a gentle wave of beams of love coming from his angel's penetrating gaze. He felt the angel touch his forearm, almost like a whisper of breath, gently acknowledging Joshua's thankfulness.

"Although I have been with you since your birth, God has allowed you to actually see me now for the very first time," Joshua's guardian said.

The angel's demeanor shifted to child-like exuberance. "You always believed without seeing. You were eager to know about angels from children's books you used to read long ago. Do you remember sneaking a flashlight into your room, and when all were asleep, you would read—sometimes into the early morning hours when your parents slept?"

Joshua nodded silently while a wisp of memory floated by. He had the image of a small log cabin bedroom where he, as a young, vital youth, would eagerly turn the book's pages. The only illumination was from the flashlight he read with while being covered under the thick, green blanket that kept him warm.

"Even though you've not seen me until now, I heard the name you gave me when you were a child. You would call me Grady, the hard-working angel on your behalf."

"I still do, because you had your work cut out for you when it came to me," Joshua chuckled.

"I have come for you now, Joshua." The angel radiated light, expressing his own joy for the physical encounter about to pass between them for the first time.

As Joshua gazed upon his angel, he felt a surge of pure joy and could no longer hold back.

He fell to his knees, tears blurring his vision. His angel was sending him all the bountiful love his Creator had for him and all His other earthly children. Then, a deep, calming silence, like a warm blanket, eased Joshua's emotions.

The angel spoke lovingly, but firmly. "Stand up, Joshua! Look at this fork in the road before you." The angel grasped Joshua's forearm to help him stand up and continued. "The road to your left represents the journey from your past to the present. It shows your life as you live it on the dairy farm. The other road, to the right, seems to stretch so far, you can't even see where it ends."

Joshua was amazed at the clarity with which he was seeing. It wasn't just a "physical seeing." He was now viewing with the clarity of unearthly vision.

The road on the left showed clips of his life. Even though it was a hard road at times, it was still alive with past memories and present experiences working with the land and seeing family and friends. All these situations, he realized now, had helped enrich his heart and strengthen his soul.

Next, Joshua glanced to his right and noticed that road was clean and uncluttered, radiating a type of unearthly beauty all its own. Joshua now recognized that it had not yet been traveled upon.

Deep within, Joshua felt an intense pull—tugging him toward that unchartered path. He took in a full breath, clutched his chest, and knew he was about to walk along that road, and was ready to take that journey.

"If I'm meant to take that road to the right, I have a feeling it is going to get me where I really need to be." Joshua said.

"Are you ready?" the angelic spirit asked.

"Yes," said Joshua. "Will you walk with me?"

His angel gazed into Joshua's eyes with divine, tender love, and said nothing. The guardian simply reached for Joshua's hand.

Joshua was found late the next morning lying dead at the fork in the road. Archer, his devoted farmhand found him, having driven out to visit his friend. Archer was at the fork of the road, ready to take the left toward the farm when he saw Joshua lying on the ground.

Shocked, Archer slammed on his brakes, bringing the truck to a screeching halt.

"Josh… Josh!" Archer bellowed, jumping out of the vehicle and racing towards Joshua's still body. But it was too late. Joshua had died from a sudden heart attack—at that fork in the road.

Archer knelt down; his muscular body bent over Joshua's. It was then he noticed that Joshua's plaid shirt and coveralls were still moist with early morning dew.

Some weeks later, in parts of Ada County, Idaho, Joshua's friends and family were still talking about what had happened. Joshua's body was lying in a white-satin and bronze, flower-covered open casket. Those who witnessed the body just couldn't get over the serene look and obvious smile on Joshua's face.

Also, and as plain as day, Joshua's right hand lay there slightly clenched—as if he were holding someone else's hand in his.

> *"Never travel faster than your guardian angel can fly."*
> —St. Teresa of Calcutta
> (Mother Teresa)

A Street Lamp and the Perfect Stranger

SARAH SAT ALONE on the bench next to the street lamp. It was a chilly winter evening in the quaint village of Shadow Falls, in northeastern Ohio. As she looked down at the snow beneath her boots and felt the soft occasional snowflake on her cheek, Sarah was thankful it wasn't at all unbearably cold.

"I'll get past this," she told herself, as she brushed the tears away.

To keep warm, she tucked her purple knitted scarf more snugly around her long brown hair. Sarah had walked about a mile and a half before finding a bench to sit on. The street lamp cast a soft golden glow.

"I can't believe how alone I feel," she muttered to herself while placing her hand over her coat, trying to soothe her stomach. She was so upset.

"I can't take this!" Sarah called out in the dark. "Here I am, twenty-eight-years old, and I'm still not getting married."

No one was around or walking nearby to hear her, but it didn't matter. Sarah felt free enough to shout out the words if she wanted to. Her emotions were frayed so talking out loud helped.

Every time Sarah recalled her fiancé telling her she had driven him away, she became anxious and upset. She would force herself to breathe in and out slowly to try to calm down, but it didn't work very well. Sarah just could not get a grip on herself.

"Brad said everything was my fault!" Sarah cried out in tearful defiance. She cringed every time she thought about how he would criticize her and then be nice—then distance her, and then draw her close.

"I wasn't perfect, that's for sure. But I know I wasn't the way he made me out to be!".

Angrily, she took the handkerchief from inside her leather glove and wiped her nose. Sarah thought she loved Brad. She had tried, but if she was to be totally honest with herself, she knew something was missing.

"I thought I loved him, but maybe I really didn't." Sarah softly chided herself and sighed heavily. She realized that she, too, played a part in the relationship going wrong.

"God, I don't know if I can handle this, so please help me." Sarah breathed out another sigh and stuffed the handkerchief back inside her glove.

"I heard that," came the sound of a voice behind her.

The sound startled Sarah, as she turned quickly toward that voice. She felt embarrassed for having talked to herself out loud, because she thought she was sure no one was around.

"Excuse me, but where are you?" Sarah was looking intently through the dim light of the street lamp, trying to locate the person.

"I'm right here," a tall handsome man said, as he slowly approached the bench. "Don't be afraid. I just couldn't help but overhear what you just said."

"Actually, it wasn't to me. I was talking to God," Sarah responded firmly. After all, she wasn't sure of this man's intentions, nor had she ever seen him before.

"No one better to talk to than God," the stranger affirmed.

"Mind if I sit down here on the bench, too?" he asked, stepping forward into the light of the street lamp.

Sarah was struck first by his handsome, charismatic presence and friendly smile. She then noticed he was around five feet, eleven inches. He wasn't wearing a hat or cap. His thick and wavy flaxen hair caught her attention. It seemed to softly glisten beneath the light of the street lamp.

He stood confident and sounded mature, yet his face had a youthful appearance. She figured him to be in his mid-thirties. Under the street lamp's glow, his skin coloring shone like smooth ivory. If Sarah wasn't feeling spent from having cried so much, she would have been interested and charmed by his good looks.

She could sense deep down that whoever this man was, he wouldn't harm her in any way and motioned for him to sit down. As he sat down on the opposite end of the bench, Sarah felt a sense of ease that calmed her swirling emotions.

"Odd, that I suddenly feel more at ease in this person's presence," Sarah thought, as she quickly assessed him.

"I'm sorry, but I won't be very good company at the moment. So, perhaps it's best you might find someone else to talk to." Suddenly feeling an inescapable attraction, Sarah looked away from his gaze.

"I can tell you're not in a mood to be social, but I don't mind. If that's okay, I'd still like to sit a little while."

He was a gentleman. Her intuition was sure of it. Still, Sarah only reluctantly acknowledged it was okay for him to sit on that same bench with her.

"Surprising, isn't it? Even though it can be a cold winter evening, if one's attention is not on that, then suddenly it doesn't feel so cold." The handsome man smiled as he turned to look at her.

Sarah was somewhat taken aback after letting her hazel-colored eyes give him a darting glance. With only the soft golden glow of the lamp light near her, she still couldn't miss his gaze. She also knew he was right. Sarah wasn't aware of the cold or being upset.

"What's your name?" Sarah asked.

"Sam Carpenter," he answered while smoothing out his tan winter topcoat.

"I'm sorry, but you don't look like a Sam." Sarah tried to make light conversation, but really wasn't into it.

"Oh, it's short for Samuel. Does the name match the look now?" He offered a comforting smile.

"Actually, it does." She quipped, as his warm smile began to lift her bruised spirits.

"The name Samuel also reminds me…takes me back to Old Testament stories," Sarah said, shifting her gaze for the moment toward the snow-covered ground.

"Well, if that's the case, then I consider it a compliment to be called Samuel. However, most know me by Sam. I prefer that because it's short and to the point." He nodded with that fact and confidently reached out to offer a gloved handshake.

"I'm Sarah Greene." Inconspicuously wiping the last tear away from her eye, she turned toward him and took his hand. His grasp was firm, yet it also felt inviting and supportive. Something silently magnetic was felt by both. Yet neither said a word.

Sarah pulled back from his gentle grasp and reached into her coat pockets to keep her gloved hands warm. In her right pocket is when she felt the letter she had angrily grabbed earlier as she walked out the door. It was a letter Sarah had written over five years ago, which she also hid away, and forgot about. It was a letter to the Lord and about the right relationship. She intended to read it at some point during her current walk.

Feeling the edges of the crinkled paper caused Sarah's attention to drift away from Sam's presence. She tried to hide the fidgeting.

Sam looked over at her, noticing she was staring down at her coat pocket. "Is everything okay?" he asked, not sure why she was doing that.

"Uh…oh, it's fine!" She quickly took her hand out of her coat pocket.

"Do you live near here?" Sarah focused her attention back to him, not only because she realized she was beginning to like him, but to hide the emotions she was feeling from her recent breakup.

"About 20 minutes or so away," Sam answered. "I drove part way, and then pulled into the Commons Plaza parking lot. Something inside just made me feel like I needed to take a walk. And now, here I am, sitting next to a very pretty woman who seems sad." Sam's tone was steady and truthful. He was genuinely concerned, and his penetrating gaze didn't miss a thing; even though he knew that Sarah thought it did.

"I didn't mean to pry," Sam continued, "But as I mentioned before, I couldn't help overhearing your vocal conversation with God. Is there anything I can do to help?"

He couldn't believe it himself but just then, feelings of tenderness and attraction caught Sam off guard. Like a magnet, he was emotionally pulled toward her. At that moment, all he wanted to do was reach out, wrap his arms around her and give her a comforting hug; he kept those thoughts to himself.

Sarah felt drawn to his presence. There was something that seemed oddly familiar about him. It took her by surprise. She felt her face flush at his sincere compliment of her being pretty and hoped he wouldn't notice.

"Strange," she said out loud, cutting off his query of help. "I'm sorry for interrupting you, but I just had a distracting thought. Did you ever get the impression you felt like you knew someone or may have met them before, even if you never have?"

Sarah, seated on that park bench, looked up at Sam. She wanted to know. She just didn't want it to seem obvious she was wondering that about the two of them.

"Yeah, I understand what you mean." Sam chuckled. His warm smile widened because he was sensing the same thing about her without wanting to say it.

"May I ask what you do for a living?" Sarah posed the question, nervously shuffling snow back and forth with her boot knowing that Sam had silently caught on to why she changed the subject.

"I'm an architect and contractor, but in my spare time, I really like being out in nature. And you?" he asked, his inviting gaze focused on how truly pretty Sarah was.

"I own the flower shop in the village. My shop is the only one there."

"What's it called?" Sam asked.

"Dreaming Flower Studio," Sarah answered, looking directly at him. "I sell various flower bouquets—with or without vases—and plants of the region. I also conduct or sponsor other people who teach how to make different types of arrangements. I've got a back classroom area for that. I have other things there, too…"

Sarah abruptly stopped talking, not wanting to go on and on about her small business which she could discuss all day. She was a contemporary young woman who really enjoyed her calling. Sarah was able to 'whistle while she worked' at something she was happy doing which also brought joy to others.

"I'm impressed, flower girl—with or without vases."

Sam's lighthearted tone of acknowledged accomplishment caused Sarah to smile rather than feel offended.

"Ah, hah! I caught that beam; don't try to hide it," Sam said, knowing his respectful humor caused her to perk up. He couldn't help but want to make her smile.

"I'm smitten by your smile!" Sam became dramatic by pressing his hand against his chest, as if shot by Cupid's arrow. He slouched left toward her.

"Cut it out!" Sarah playfully poked his shoulder, thinking to herself how easy it was to be with this perfect stranger who didn't feel like one at all.

"Seriously, from what you tell me, Sarah, you have accomplished a dream of yours. It's not surprising then you have the word 'dream' as part of the name of your studio."

"Good for you!" Sam said, sitting upright again, still sensing that magnetic pull toward her.

"You know, it's getting colder now. Would you like to grab a cup of coffee with me?" Sam was secretly hoping he wouldn't feel disappointed if Sarah said "No".

Trying to escape the butterfly feeling in her gut, Sarah scooted a little further away from him—toward the other end of the bench. She was surprised her upset stomach was gone. Still, she was a little hesitant as to what to answer. After all, Sarah didn't want to end up with yet another heartache should this become more than just having a cup of coffee.

Sam patiently waited for an answer.

Sarah decided to take a chance.

"Okay, I've got time this evening. I'll have a cup of coffee with you, Sam."

They stood up together. Sam's cell phone rang.

"Hello, Sam here," he was saying as he walked a short distance away to take the call.

Brushing some snowflakes from her coat, Sarah again heard the crinkling of the paper in her pocket. It was that letter she had written and found; the one she angrily grabbed earlier on her way out the door.

She pulled the paper from her right pocket and read it while waiting for Sam. She could feel her pulse quicken and her mouth drop.

Sarah had written a more detailed description of the man she had hoped for. It was the man of her dreams, one who did not exist, but she hoped one day would. What she had written did not fit the attributes or physical description of Brad, her former fiancé. It was the description of Sam—right down to his walks in nature.

"This is unbelievable!"

Sarah was truly stunned. Even in the colder weather, she felt heat flushing her face when she turned to look at the image of Sam standing in the distance and talking on his cell phone.

"Just a minute Carl," Sam said to the caller and took the cell phone away from his ear.

"Hey Sarah, it's a client," he murmured walking back toward her, holding his hand over the phone. "I'll just be a minute—and only that—it's getting brisk out here." He laughed and gave her a quick wink.

"Well, I'm game if You are…I will try one more time…We'll see." Sarah prayed as she looked up to the night sky talking quietly to the Lord.

"Shall we?" Having finished the call, he gestured for her to walk beside him while they crossed the street and headed to the café. Sam's green-eyed gaze cast in her direction was more captivating to her than she thought. It silenced her.

Sarah remained quiet as they walked along. Feeling the firm and stable grasp of Sam's hand, she thought back to the letter, wondering if it could be true. What she didn't know, however, was that sometime back, Sam had also requested the exact same thing--to be with the person truly meant for him.

"The inner voice is something which cannot be described in words. But sometimes we have a positive feeling that something in us prompts us to do a certain thing. The time when I learnt to recognize this voice was, I may say, the time when I started praying regularly."
—Mahatma Gandhi

An Angel Dressed in Cowboy Boots

PAUL AND AL, really good friends since 3rd grade, decided to go horseback riding in southern Ohio, not far from the state forest there. Initially, neither one of them knew how to ride very well. Their first experiences were those occasional ones which were hour jaunts at a riding stable during summers in high school. But, after a while, they both went more and more often and became pretty good basic riders. Now in their early forties, both men sat horseback in western saddles, leisurely guiding their horses up the winding trail while reminiscing about the old days.

Paul, in faded blue jeans and grey cotton shirt, rode a twelve-year-old white Arab gelding, bred for its calmness and surefootedness on the trails. Its nickname was 'Cedar'. Paul's thick, dark hair was pulled into a small ponytail at the back of his neck. His dark sunglasses rested comfortably underneath a black Navy Vet cap.

"Go figure that one," Al said as he called out Cedar's name. Al clucked to Paul's horse to move up closer so he could talk to Paul better.

"The color of your horse is white. Uh, why is he nicknamed Cedar?" Al asked, looking over his shoulder, his own thick brown hair cut to above the collar of his black, long sleeved cotton shirt. Al pushed some of it away from the collar after shooing a fly that had decided to join them.

"Knucklehead, look closer at his fur," Paul said, chuckling. "He has cedar-colored speckles on him, that's why, and quit trying to tell my horse what to do!" Both looked at each other and laughed as they always did—each liking to needle one another in friendship.

These two young men had more than a few things in common and were true friends. Paul Cattoneo and Al Angelo were similar in height with Paul being slightly taller, around five feet, ten inches. They both liked to talk politics, experience adventures together, and to party hardy when they could. Both were also responsible small business owners. They both enjoyed a good meal together, too, whether it be a good steak dinner or a full plate of homemade pasta with spaghetti sauce.

"At least my horse has marked colors and definition," Al said, laughing in playful competition, as he reached in the pocket of his khaki-colored pants to retrieve a piece of candy. Al's horse was a nine-year-old Appaloosa named Patches with beautiful black and brown patches that seemed exquisitely painted and artfully in place against the white fur on the mare's body.

Sure-footed horses, like these two, were required for the terrain both men chose to ride even if it was at a slower, leisurely pace. They both liked animals and considered these horses to be 'their relations' in a way—both human and horse, looking out for each other.

"Home, home on the range, where the deer and the antelope…" Paul started to sing, but then stopped short and said, "Here we are two Italian cowboys, just a moseying through this beautiful wooded, country setting. I wonder if there were any real Italian cowboys in the American West way back then?"

"Uh, yes," Al retorted. "Haven't you ever seen a spaghetti western movie? You know, some of the old classics that were filmed in Italy?" Paul remembered and both laughed out loud, hearing the echo of their laughter reverberate through that canyon-like trail and dense underbrush.

Suddenly, they heard rustling sounds in the thicker patches of the underbrush, so Paul and Al stopped their horses.

"Where is the movement coming from exactly? How far is it, can you tell?" Al's voice lowered as he questioned Paul. Al was very uneasy and didn't have a good feeling about this.

Just then, both heard the distant low snarl of a big cat, and Paul could tell by the sound it wasn't a bobcat. He knew instinctively it must be a cougar.

"This can't be what I think it is, can it?" Paul responded as if talking to himself as well as Al. "I'm pretty sure it's a cougar, and it's close!" Paul motioned to Al. "Let's get out of here!"

Paul tried to guide his horse back around, but his horse balked, because out of nowhere, a cougar lunged forward from the under-brush—right at Al. It all happened so fast.

"Al! Watch out!" Paul yelled. He could tell it was a male predator and looked to be every bit of 200 pounds or more.

"What?" Al quickly turned his head to the right. He couldn't believe what he was seeing. A look of shock covered his face.

Al couldn't act fast enough. His horse was neighing and snorting loudly, its head twisting back and forth trying to escape the bit and get away, but the cougar launched itself up too fast. Its massive paws were swiping at Al. Fortunately, the cougar missed its mark and fell backward.

"I can't hold on! God, please help me!" Al cried out when the Appaloosa suddenly reared up, trying to strike at the cougar.

Al fell from the saddle, and Patches ran off—a small cloud of dust from the dirt trail following behind.

The cougar, its tawny color blending in with the undertone of the dirt trail, was breathing heavily. It was temporarily stunned from the fall and the missed target.

"No!" Paul called out as he heard that low snarl again and watched as the cougar slowly brought his head up.

"Cedar, move!" Paul commanded, as his scared and agitated horse pushed forward by Paul having squeezed Cedar's sides with his heels. While trying to keep control, Paul positioned his own horse in between Al and the cougar—a hedge of protection.

"God, I hope you're listening. Help us." Al said the words quietly, as he struggled to his feet, but loud enough that he knew Paul could hear.

"I'm in trouble. I think I'm going to be lunch!" Al said in surprise. He suddenly wanted to run but remembered that running away is the worst thing one can do. Al felt his heart thumping hard. Danger and fear were colliding with his feigned attempt at humor.

Paul's mind raced, not only because of the cougar's surprise attack, but by Al's short, quick prayer, because Al once told Paul that he was angry at God.

"Stay where you are!" Paul said sharply. "I'm going to shoot!" Both Paul and Al had gun licenses. Al rarely wore a pistol on his person, but Paul's gun was holstered on his right hip and hidden.

Paul quickly reached for his weapon while trying hard to hold onto his scared, snorting and stomping horse. He saw the cougar with its muscled body ready to launch another attack. Paul aimed and was ready to shoot.

Just then a tall, slim male appeared from around the bend of the trail. He ran toward them.

"Don't shoot! I got this!" the mysterious man called out.

The slender male had light brown hair and chiseled looking facial features with startling blue, yet compassionate eyes. He had a mildly tan complexion and a demeanor of calm strength and easy attitude. Paul quickly assessed that he looked to be in his early forties.

"Steady boy, easy now…" The man moved effortlessly, as he came up behind the cougar, talking to it. Startled, the cougar turned toward the man, its lips curled, fanged teeth showing. Yet, the cougar did not attack.

The man stood there and looked into the large cat's eyes. Normally this would be a threat to the cougar, but somehow there was no apparent risk. It was as if the two were communicating somehow. That was evident and plain to see by both Paul and Al.

The large wild cat, breathing hard, quieted down. Its loud snarl faded to a low growl. Its tense and readied stance shifted to one of escape. Without any clue, the cougar suddenly ran past the man and back into the deep underbrush.

"Phew! That was a close call," the man called out to both men, as he straightened out the arms of his white western-looking shirt. "He won't be botherin' either of you again. Thank goodness I didn't have to get my clothes dirty—especially my boots. I really like these comfortable leather ranchers." His smile became more evident as he walked closer.

"The name's Shane," he said, dusting off his pale-colored blue jeans and then his cowboy boots.

Both men were completely surprised by what they had just witnessed. Neither knew what to say at first. Al just stood there, still shaken, while Paul continued to hold his gun and tried to calm the Arab he was riding. Paul wasn't sure whether to holster the pistol yet—or not.

"Okay, you can both relax now," Shane said, as he walked a little closer to them, then stopped.

"And would you be so kind as to put the gun away?" Shane shifted his focus to Paul. "I know why you have it. But I'm wonderin' if you really need it." Shane shrugged his shoulders and with a warm smile said, "I'm thinkin' the good Lord doesn't think you do."

"Well, if you think you're sure." Paul looked toward that underbrush first. He didn't hear any sound or see any brush moving, so he withdrew his gun and holstered it.

"I am as certain as I'm standing here." Shane's words were reassuring. There was such a calm presence about him.

"It would be good for the two of you to get a little more history about these parts of the woods before you ride next time. It's not as tame as one might think," Shane said, giving a wink.

"Well nice meeting the two of you, brief as it was. I'll be on my way now." With that, Shane simply turned on the heels of his boots and began walking away.

Paul and Al both noticed the soft, but definite golden hue that seemed to encircle this man, right down to the leather roper rancher boots. The sun's rays were also right behind him, beaming down through the trees.

"It was most probably just the sun rays that surrounded him like that," Paul said to Al.

"Where did you come from, and I can't thank you enough! You saved me from being attacked!" Al said, calling out to Shane.

Paul responded with his thanks as well. He felt like he wanted to urge his horse to walk toward Shane, so he could find out more about him, but something inside himself seemed to whisper, "No, you're not to go".

"I came from over there a ways." Shane spoke louder, as he pointed a finger out in front of him and continued to walk away. "I heard you had called for help, and you are both welcome."

"What? Who told you? How could you have known we needed help?" Al tossed out each question with a loud voice, as he watched the tall, slim figure heading even further away. "How could he have known that?" Al turned to Paul, completely taken aback.

Al gently urged his horse forward a few steps and called out again for Shane to wait. However, Shane was already around that bend in the trail. He was gone.

"How could he have heard? He wasn't anywhere near us." Al said, turning back around toward Paul.

"Al, you did ask the Lord for help. I heard you."

In the blink of an eye, it dawned on the both of them what had just happened.

"Wow!" They both said it together at the same time. Al felt especially grateful and humbled by the experience.

"By the way, your horse didn't bolt away. You'll find him on the way back," Shane's voice carried through the distance.

"Shane!" Paul shouted. "Thanks again for your help!"

Nothing but nature's silence was the response.

Back at the stable, Paul and Al told their story to the manager, Jake. He was a stocky, but sturdy looking older man who had been working at this stable for well over 7 years. Jake took very good care of the horses. It was an honest living he truly enjoyed.

"So, you saw him, too, and he helped you?" Jake's intentional gaze lay focused on the two of them as he posed the question.

"Yeah!" Al spoke first. "Who is he?"

"You mean, who was he?" Jake responded with an air of mystery behind the words. "What does that mean?" Paul asked.

"Well, you just gave the full description, right down to the clothes and boots of Shane Mack. He died on that trail some years back."

"Oh, come on, you can't be serious, Jake, and I know you don't take us for fools either!" Paul retorted and became momentarily agitated, thinking that Jake was just pulling their legs.

"I am as serious as a heartbeat, and I can tell you sir, it is real." Jake said with a cool, firm response.

"Look I'm sorry for acting a bit sarcastic." Paul ran his fingers through his hair, "but you've got to understand, this is pretty unbelievable!"

Paul's apology was accepted because Jake understood that Paul's reaction was the same type he had come across before. Jake recalled silently how many times that he had to say the same thing to others and had received the same type of response—at first. Yet, it was all true.

"How did he die?" Al asked.

"It happened in that unfamiliar territory you boys rode up into and weren't supposed to. But then again, quite a few people over the years have done the same thing, and quite a few of them got into trouble." Jake sat down on a bale of hay outside the barn and continued. "Those who got into a serious jam were always helped by a guy named Shane who fit the same description, right down to those rancher boots," Jake said, motioning Paul and Al to sit on the two hard back chairs nearby.

Both men followed each other to the chairs. They were intently listening to this amazing story, urging Jake to keep talking.

"The story goes that Shane was riding up the northern quadrant on that trail, same as you told me you did, and he came near and around an open cavern area near a bend in the trail. His horse got real fidgety and scared. He quieted his horse, and that is when he spotted a wounded cougar on that trail."

Jake repositioned the bale of hay so he could lean his back up against the barn door. The sun was warm and comforting. Jake always felt best in this kind of weather.

Paul and Al looked at each other, both of their mouths dropped open when they heard the word 'cougar', but Al spoke first. "This is unbelievable!"

Jake put his hand up in a gesture that asked for patience while he continued. "So, Shane brought his horse up as far as he could, because his ride was getting a bit nervous. He quieted the horse and dismounted. Now normally, Shane's horse wouldn't go anywhere, but not that day. When his horse came closer to that cougar, wounded or not, it bolted back, got loose from Shane and ran off."

The manager pushed up the sleeves of his thin knit pullover sweater and kept talking. "They said Shane was alone on that trail with a badly wounded cougar, which anybody knows is not a good deal at all because you don't know whether that animal would attack or not."

Jake shifted his sitting position and reached down for the glass of lemonade he had waiting for him. He took a sip or two and continued.

"Anyway, Shane must have taken his chances because talk is he tried to help that cougar. Talk goes they found one of Shane's new rancher boots, with water in it, lying next to the body of the dead cougar. The cougar's mouth was wet, as if it had taken some sips of that water from Shane's boot."

"What happened to Shane after he helped the cougar?" Paul asked, getting up from the chair. He wanted to know what happened to Shane, trying to mentally digest what had been said so far.

"They never found Shane's body, only evidence of a pretty bad struggle. The speculation is Shane must have somehow gone over the cliff on the right side of the trail, near where the cougar had lain and fell headlong into that rushing river. Nobody knows for sure. They could tell from the investigation though, that the evidence of whatever struggle it was, may not have happened between Shane and that cougar!" Jake concluded the story and drank more of the cold lemonade.

Al and Paul were literally speechless at this point. They didn't know what to say to each other or to this storyteller sitting in front of them.

Jake, on the other hand, was used to stunned silences. He had experienced those before, many times. So, he decided to keep talking.

"Wanna' know my thoughts, boys?" Jake asked after having put the empty glass back down on the ground.

"Yeah, we want to know," Paul said.

"I think he struggled with the person who shot that cougar. You see, no one is supposed to be up that way hunting for sport. There was shootin' for sport up there and burglaries a few times, too! It was big trouble to do that stuff and get caught, especially back then, and I think Shane knew who it was."

Jake stood up, twisted his upper body back and forth to stretch out his back muscles then stepped closer to Paul and Al. He lowered his voice as if to convey something more confidential.

"Anyway, when Shane went riding that day, one of his friends told the police he had on a white western type of shirt, blue jeans and those new rancher boots. They never did get enough evidence to find out exactly who or what caused Shane to go over that cliff—if in fact, that's what happened."

"This is incredible! And, if we hadn't seen him ourselves, we wouldn't have believed it!" Al did not even attempt to hide his bewildered amazement.

Al, rocking back and forth on that hard back chair was so intent on listening that he wasn't paying attention. That's when he rocked the chair a little too far. It fell backward, and he almost slipped off, but caught himself.

"Please, not again!" Paul said, half laughing, referring to Al having fallen from his horse, and now just missed from falling—again. Even though Paul joked, he hid the shakiness he was also feeling because of the story and having seen Shane.

"We saw him. He was wearing the same clothes, right down to those boots! I can't believe this. We really saw a spirit, and one who helped us." Al's attitude brightened.

Paul, though, could not fit the pieces together. He was a practical kind of guy. Although he believed in the afterlife, he just couldn't get his head wrapped around the fact that who he thought was a live, physical person, was actually a spirit who had helped them. Paul was slowly shaking his head back and forth as he looked down, shuffling the dirt with the bottom of his right boot.

"Oh, believe it, boys!" Jake snapped back emphatically. "Shane Mack has helped many since his passing. I wouldn't be surprised if he has received his 'wings' by now. Know what I mean?" Jake flashed a smile and continued. "Shane was a really good guy to people and animals."

Jake turned back around to get the bale of hay. As he slung it off to the side, he glanced back over his shoulder at the two men.

"It's another reason why we usually get a bunch of people come to talk and ride here at Sundown Stables. It's also why sometimes we don't. Some people just can't handle the experience."

Jake grinned, his teeth even and white against his tan, weathered skin. "Well, nice meetin' you both. I've got to get back to work. I hope to see you again—if you're not too afraid to come back." Jake started to walk away, but abruptly stopped and turned back toward them.

"Oh, by the way, that horse of Shane's, well, he never did bolt away. They found him about a mile back up the road. The horse seemed like it was waiting for Shane to come get him. That horse and Shane were a team."

"While I'm thinking about it," Jake said, brushing sweat away from his forehead, "It also seems to me that Shane somehow knew you boys needed help too, just like the others. You know, it's a lesson for all of us. Life goes on and on and on," Jake concluded, as he waved a good-bye and headed back toward the paddock.

That last piece of truth about the horse and help, well, it was all just over the top for both Al and Paul. They headed to the car in total silence. The only sounds made came from the gravel stones underneath their boots as they walked.

Suddenly, Al turned to Paul and said, "Paul, it's true, I really did ask God for help this time, and I meant it!"

"I know, I know." Paul reassured, remembering the short prayer called out loud just before the cougar was ready to attack.

"And it's also true, that right after, Shane appeared. Right?" Al asked for that confirmation all the while shaking his head in awe of what had occurred.

"Yes, it was right after you asked for help." Paul agreed.

Without another word spoken, both men knew that a prayer was heard in a miraculous way.

They got in the car and silently drove away. This experience would be remembered in their minds and hearts for a very long time.

"Every moment and every event of every man's life on earth plants something in his soul."
—THOMAS MERTON

Chrysalis to Butterfly

MARK TAPPED HIS finger restlessly against the steering wheel of the car while waiting for the light to turn green. He was in a hurry. Being a psychologist definitely had its pressures to be sure, but since he was a teenager, Mark knew counseling would be his calling. Even back then, the one thing he liked even more than football was anything related to psychology.

Looking into the rear-view mirror, Mark brushed his dark, thick hair back into place. "The wind messed it up," he thought to himself waiting for the darn light to change. He had to be at the Calm Force Health Care Center, outside Bennington, in Lamoille County, Vermont.

The light flashed green. "It's about time," he muttered, and placed his foot back on the gas pedal, slightly shifting his five foot, eight-inch muscled frame comfortably in the Honda Civic. Due to his schedule, Mark was given special morning visiting hours, and he needed to get there.

The girl was twenty-two-years old. She was a short-statured, brown-haired girl whom Mark's wife had taught in the 12th grade. Mark and his wife, Jennifer, had been friends with her ever since. Christy Camlin was always asking questions and wanted to go deeper into her being to understand more about herself.

Mark and Jennifer both saw in Christy someone "unordinary" in the sense that there was something different about her—a bright spark within her. Christy was also unconventional in her way, a bit of a free spirit too, and generally not afraid to stand up for herself. She was well liked by people who came to know her.

"Why on earth did Christy admit herself into the health care facility?" Mark quietly asked himself. All he was told by her sister who, having called, said that Christy was experiencing a sudden depression, felt insecure and was anxious. She was prescribed a low dose antidepressant and sessions with the attending psychiatrist at the Center.

"How long has she been there?" Mark asked, having called Christy's sister on his cell phone.

"About seven days," Laura, her older sister, responded.

"Why didn't she call us?" he asked with a surprised, concerned tone in his voice.

"I don't know. She didn't tell any of us in the family either when it first happened. We had to hear it from the attending psychiatrist that she had admitted herself and she didn't want to be seen at first either," Laura explained with a hint of irritation in her voice.

The short conversation was not surprising because Mark did know that Christy's older sister was not close to her. Although there were a few reasons, the 9-year age difference, being one of them, prevented some of that closeness from happening.

Mark called his wife, Jennifer, to let her know he had arrived at the Center.

"Honey, in general, did you notice anything out of place with Christy? Was she not acting herself in any way?" Mark was concerned and needed to know.

"No, Mark, I didn't. I really didn't. She just seemed a little quieter than her usual bubbly self," Jennifer said.

"Hmm. I didn't notice anything either, but when you said she seemed a little quieter than her normal "bubbly" self, that may have presented one of the clues. Love you, Jen, gotta' go. I'm right at the front door of the Center."

"Okay, love you too. Call me when you leave." Jennifer made the sound of a kiss over the phone before hanging up.

On his way in, Mark wondered if this episode of Christy's came on suddenly. "She must be sensing something she can't even explain to herself." Mark's thoughts traveled across his mind as he approached the reception area.

"Christy Camlin," Mark stated, letting the nurse at the desk know he was one of the visitors. "Oh, hello Dr. Wade," came the nurse's response, having recognized him. She looked down at the roster. "Here you are," she said, as she checked off his name on the visitor's schedule. "Right this way." The tall, uniformed nurse left the reception station and led him to the visiting lounge area.

"There she is, and already better." The nurse nodded and smiled. "In fact, she is helping other patients by talking with them! We all like her." With that, she turned and headed back to her station.

Christy was sitting quietly on the brown leather couch, looking out the large bay window. There, attached to the full, white-flowered milkweed, Christy had spotted a chrysalis from which a butterfly would soon emerge. She was fascinated with what she was seeing. The hard, protective shell had already been there when she arrived at the Center. How long would it take, Christy didn't know, but she was hoping she would be able to see that butterfly break free.

Interestingly enough, just before she admitted herself into the hospital, Christy had been researching how butterflies develop and learned about the four stages—egg, caterpillar, chrysalis and butterfly. It was amazing to her how these stages of metamorphosis could occur. To her, it was a miracle all its own.

Christy would go to the lounge area daily, sit and look out the window. She watched and hoped she would see the butterfly emerge. Sitting there on the soft brown leather sofa looking at the hanging chrysalis helped her to feel calmer, emotionally cushioned. For now, this was her own protected corner of her world.

"Hi, Christy!" Mark called out to her.

Christy was so focused looking out the window at this phenomenon, she didn't notice him.

The sound of his voice surprised her, causing her to quickly turn toward him.

"Oh, hello Mark, I didn't see you," she said, tightening the twisty which was holding her thick, chestnut hair ponytail in place. Mark and his wife, having become friends with Christy, bypassed any formal names or titles.

"Why didn't you call us?" Mark asked, his face showing concern, as he bent over to give her a hug.

"That tan looks good on you," was how she responded. "I guess you and Jennifer had some time to get some sun out west while you were at your psychology conference." Christy knew full well she was evading the question.

"Christy, you're not answering." Mark wouldn't let her get away with it.

"Why didn't you call?"

"And what would you have been able to do?" she asked, shifting her position on the comfortable sofa. "You and Jennifer were out of state, and I didn't want to interrupt your conference." Christy was sincere. She really didn't want to cause a problem for them.

"Christy, in this case, it was an emergency. We are your friends." Mark was patient with his words, but his tone carried a worried edge.

"I know, and I'm sorry. I didn't mean to worry you or anyone. But I just couldn't bring myself to tell anyone that I, of all people, was feeling down or having an anxiousness of sorts. I was embarrassed," she said. Christy sighed heavily, and continued talking, the confused look in her eyes was evident.

"I don't know what happened. I just felt low, and I was anxious. On top of it, I had so much on my mind, I just couldn't concentrate very well—at all."

Christy tilted her head away from his gaze. She didn't want Mark to see the tears she was forcing herself to hold back.

"Embarrassed?" Mark questioned. "Why would you feel that way? It happens to a lot of people. That's nothing to feel embarrassed about, Christy. It's okay, it really is."

"Maybe to you, it's okay, but to me, it's not. People see me as a confident, optimistic person who seems to be able to handle anything. I don't even know what's happening or why. Do you think other people would?" Christy started to nervously tap her foot on the carpeted floor.

"I felt like I was breaking down in some ways inside, and yet it's like I'm struggling to break out, break free!" Christy was becoming anxious. Her hands began to tremble, and she could feel heat rushing up to her face. She suddenly felt caged.

"Christy, relax. It's okay. Just take a few slow, gentle deep breaths— in and out. Breathe in…breathe out." Mark instructed her, as he sat down beside her. She followed his words and began the rhythmic breathing. She immediately felt the relief.

"Some people say that anxiety can be related to fear of the future in some way," she said, looking at Mark with her luminous forest green eyes. She waited for his response.

"Do you feel afraid of the future, Christy?"

"I don't know…I mean … I just finished college. I'll be graduating soon and ready to start living my life, right? I should be happy, but I'm not." Christy pushed up the sleeves of her sweater and sighed again.

"Maybe it's because I feel like there won't be any more stability. Is that it? Maybe that's it," Christy said, her words trailing off, the uncertainty apparent.

"You mean, are you afraid there won't be any more security, or stability—that sense of feeling cushioned within the walls of college dorms and college life in general? You'll be out on your own and that makes you anxious?" Mark asked, touching the back of her hand. He patiently waited for a response.

Christy slowly looked upward toward Mark's brown-eyed stare. It was as if a slow realization was about to emerge from within her.

"Are you nervous that your safety net of structure, community of friends and peers in that college life you've lived will be unraveling? You'll feel like you're out in the world all by yourself?" Mark questioned her gently, but persistently.

Suddenly, as if a huge light bulb of awareness just woke her up to the bright illumination of truth, Christy blurted out, "Oh my gosh, yes, could that be a good part of it? I am scared that I'm not confident enough to walk out into the world on my own!" Christy heard herself say the revealing words, but for just that moment had trouble believing it herself. Even more awareness was now flooding from her mind into more words she wanted to communicate.

"I mean, when I think about it, even though I am on my own, I'm not and haven't been really. Since I was six years old, other than summers, all I've known is school." Christy's expressive hand gestures made the surprised awareness even more evident.

"I've been cushioned in a bubble of education, content to be there. I felt secure, because I was with groups of peers, friends and people all doing the same thing—going to school. There is the security of structure, too. The class schedules gave me that. All of it was a sense of belonging." Christy said, looking at Mark.

Without need for explanation, her green eyes widened. There was a momentary pause—silence. She just stared at Mark, seemingly frozen for a moment in time—her mind working rapidly to pull thoughts together to form the idea, the clear realization of truth.

Suddenly, Christy jumped up from her sitting position on the couch. "Oh my gosh, that's it! I'm scared to be alone. I'll walk out after graduation. I'll pretend I enjoy the parties, the hugs, and the promises of seeing friends often."

She started pacing back and forth, intent on the realization that she felt was just at the rim—gaining speed from her subconscious toward her consciousness. She could feel her heart begin to race, the light bulb of the reason why she felt anxious ready to click on.

"Then, when all is said and done, I'm picturing myself at home, alone. I'm not confident to face the next stage I'm moving into—the adult stage—and walking out into the world on my own. That's it! Now I know where the anxiety was coming from."

Christy felt the gnawing tension in the pit of her stomach dissolve into a comfortable feeling again—relief. It felt really good.

"Well, there you have it, at least more than some of it." Mark chimed the words. He had known Christy for over four years now.

He was assured by her words and actions that she had gained some true insight.

"Mark, you know, the psychiatrist I have been talking with was trying to point some of this out to me as well, but for some reason I just didn't get it!" she emphasized the words, breathed yet another sigh of relief and continued. "Since I've been here and trying to understand, I realized I just kept coming here daily, to watch the chrysalis out this window," Christy said, and pointed to where she wanted Mark to look.

"Christy, it certainly looks like the butterfly is just about ready to emerge, don't you think?" Mark pulled up the window blinds so they could both see the chrysalis even better.

"Yes, I do think that butterfly is coming out of that shell!" Christy happily acknowledged with newfound confidence in her voice.

"Mark, thank you from the bottom of my heart," Christy said. She leaned closer and gave him a hug. "I'm so grateful you helped me become aware of this. You helped me 'get it.'"

Mark smiled and said, "Now dear girl, I can tell by what you said overall, that there may also be a deeper issue you may want to address in counseling. For now, by gosh, I think you've got it!" Mark stood up, pushed back one side of his brown leather jacket, placed his hand on his hip and playfully snapped his fingers with his other hand.

"A possible breakthrough!" Christy laughed, her smile beaming. Mark was grateful to see her feeling happy again.

"Do you know why you kept being drawn to that chrysalis?" Mark asked as they both leaned over the back of the couch to again, look out the window.

At that moment, the chrysalis was moving. Both Mark and Christy watched with surprise and wonder, as the butterfly began to break through. They watched as it emerged and hung upside down. Its wings were wet but pulsing with its blood substance circulating through those beautiful colored wings. It would take a while, but after the wings were dry, off the butterfly would go—flying free.

Christy began to softly cry. These were tears caused by awareness and joy. She gazed through the window and watched the butterfly. To her, it was as if the amazing creature was saying, "You see, if I can do it, so can you. When the time is right, come fly with me."

She quickly turned her head toward Mark who was also watching through the window.

"Mark, I kept being drawn to the chrysalis because I'm the chrysalis right now and within me is emerging the butterfly. I'm struggling to break free into the next stage of living. A breakdown of sorts is really a breakthrough," Christy continued. "Like the butterfly, I connected to the weakness, the fear, and I am breaking through it to emerge," she said, wiping the tears away with a Kleenex she took from the pocket of her favorite emerald green sweater.

Mark gave her a soft kiss of acknowledgment on the forehead. It was time for him to go. He knew that very shortly, Christy herself would be leaving, too. She would be like that butterfly—emerging and flying out into the experience of life—free to create another new, secure reality.

Almost six years later, on a crisp, and sunny spring day, Mark and Jennifer's young daughter opened the door to the bookstore that everyone in town loved to visit. It certainly had character. This bookstore also came equipped with satisfaction for the taste buds as well. Coffee, tea and various community favorite hot and cold drinks, and a small variety of fresh assorted bakery and sandwiches were served. Choices of low fat, and gluten free were added to the simple, but well enjoyed menu.

The store itself was designed for a time remembered—long past when wooden shelves, counters and floors, as well as old fashioned registers, were the style and equipment of the time. It was as if the very early twentieth century of the past was brought forward into the present. Yet, it was also like feeling at home when someone entered. There was a universal, comforting atmosphere that adults, teenagers, and children alike could connect with and enjoy a past-remembered time.

There were wall-to-wall shelves of books and small round tables with soft-white embroidered linen draping over them. Beautiful, various hanging verdant green plants decorated the bookstore. A person could sit and relax at the cozy tables or on the cushioned chairs and love seats sporadically spaced throughout. It was an extremely successful, independently owned establishment, one that many people from the area hoped would be there for a very long time.

"Look Mom, Dad!" Mark and Jennifer's eight-year-old daughter, Jessica, pointed to the window. "Look how pretty the butterfly picture is and look how nice this butterfly bush is outside here. I really like it!" their daughter exclaimed, which she would do regularly before entering the bookstore.

"Yes, so do we!" Both parents responded in unison.

Jessica rushed into the bookstore, went straight for the cupcakes and milk, then to her favorite bookshelf in the specially designed children's section.

Mark and Jennifer looked over at the counter, and waved hello to Christy Camlin, owner of the Butterfly Bookstore.

Yes, Christy flew like the butterfly, found her own dream and created a new security, a new life—something she didn't think possible before. She landed in a community that truly enjoyed and accepted what she had to offer, and she received back the sweet nectar of reward.

"Christy has securely landed." Mark said to his wife while catching that first whiff of the mild book-scented fragrance.

Butterfly Bookstore had become solidly accepted and a comfortable getaway for himself, his family, and their community.

Mark closed the door behind him. He and his wife headed for the coffee and then toward their favorite section of books.

"We delight in the beauty of the butterfly, but rarely admit the changes it has gone through to achieve that beauty."
—MAYA ANGELOU

Jolt and the Journey

ALL MATT WANTED to do was run away.

"Get out! Not…be…here…anymore!" Matt ran his fingers through his thick, wavy brown hair trying to organize his angered thoughts.

"Darn it! Why should I try anymore? What difference does it make? I'm not appreciated for any of it anyway!" He took his wedding ring off and tossed it into the glove compartment of his Jeep Wrangler.

Matt considered himself a faithful and loyal person. Through thick and thin, he stayed with her. Nine years prior, when he was thirty-years-old, he had married her under God's grace in a church ceremony. He meant every word he said, too. Today he stared at his own light brown eyes in the rearview mirror, those tortured-filled eyes looking right back at him telling the story of how he was feeling.

Matt and Melissa Talbot were going to separate. "She wants it, not me," he spouted off angrily to himself. Matt had been sitting in that vehicle for a while with coffee and a now cold egg and sausage muffin with hash browns to keep him company. He couldn't eat.

Early this morning, he couldn't believe what he heard. His wife was serious when she said she had enough and was going to leave. Standing there with sport jacket in hand and ready for work, Matt recalled how stunned he felt with the news. With her words, it was like she slapped him hard in the face. He was speechless.

"Why didn't I say anything?" he said to himself, recalling the events. Matt recalled how his heart began to race and his breath quickened, as he tried to hold back the anger, which underneath, was due to his feeling so hurt. He couldn't talk.

He purchased a corner unit townhouse in Greensboro, North Carolina. It was especially for her—complete with a larger lot of partially wooded area and verdant green grass. It was a peaceful home, a retreat from the city world. However, early this morning, it was anything but serene.

Matt just walked out, slamming the front door.

He had driven to their development's community lake before going to work. Even though spring was just around the corner with signs of melting snow scattered here and there, it was still pretty chilly outside. It was quiet there though, and he knew he'd be alone to collect himself—just the way he wanted it.

Matt had a marathon-runner physique. He enjoyed swimming at the lake during the sunny, warm days. He also liked to just sit and watch the rowboats gliding by, young ones playing, and older couples walking near the shoreline holding hands. He also noticed people came there to fish, swim, cookout or just to relax.

This was a large, manmade run-off lake and was stocked with various kinds of fish. The development where Matt and Melissa lived took care of it and other "perks" of living in Sun Lit Meadows, a gated community of wealthy townhouse owners.

"I can't believe it!" Matt angrily spit the words out, as he sat in the driver's seat with clenched fists hugging the wheel. His upsetting self-talk continued. "What is going on? I just can't believe she wants to leave. I've been there for her, but she says I'm not. All I've done it seems, is work hard to support us in gaining a comfortable life." He slammed the palm of his hand against the steering wheel "What is Melissa talking about? I'm here for her!"

The sound of Matt's agonizing words bounced through the Wrangler as he reached for the food. He just couldn't do it and tossed the muffin sandwich back on the front seat.

He thought of the hidden flask of whiskey he put under the driver's seat of his vehicle, never thinking for one moment, he would get caught. It was so well hidden.

That familiar craving taunted him. He tried to ignore it and continued the heated conversation he was having with himself.

"How could she say this to me? I've spent nine years working my tail off to build my security business. I've given her a beautiful home. She didn't have to work at all if she didn't want to. How dare she say she's had enough! Well, what if I said the same thing to her?"

Even his talking out loud didn't help. The urge took hold and Matt quickly bent over, reached underneath the seat and grabbed the flask.

"Yeah, well, whether she agreed with it or not," he opened the flask and took a swig of scotch whiskey, "I have cut back on my drinking, too!" He firmly reiterated to himself.

Matt didn't think he had a drinking problem. He controlled his whiskey. He didn't drink during the week, only on the weekends. Melissa would tell him he was drinking too much, even if only on the weekends, and that if he kept it up, she would leave him. He just figured she was overreacting because Matt knew how much she loved him. He knew how much he loved her.

Matt also didn't think that having seven, or maybe eight glasses of his favorite scotch whiskey every weekend was really an issue. After all, he would say to himself, "I loaded the glass with ice, didn't I? Ah, she's just being paranoid because her brother was an alcoholic," Matt rationalized, leaning his head back against the driver's seat headrest.

"I'm not an alcoholic, and I'm not on the road to becoming one the way Melissa thinks I could be." Matt took another swig, tightly twisted the cap closed and hid the flask back underneath the seat.

Matt usually didn't carry a decanter of scotch whiskey anywhere with him. After the increasing arguments the past few weeks, and especially the one this morning, he did fill it up before he stormed out of the house. Matt wanted to have a few sips to calm his nerves.

After this morning's startling news in which Melissa delivered her brutally honest and emotional-filled opinions, Matt decided to call in to work and take the day off. It was easy to do with his owning Talbot's Security Systems. Through his enduring efforts, the company had become very successful.

"It's time to go back home," Matt said, sighing to himself after having called the company and spoke to his manager. At this moment, he didn't want to go back, but knew he should. He started the engine and adjusted the rear-view mirror. He also repositioned the rosary hanging on it, the one Melissa had given him.

Matt looked behind him and began backing out onto the two-lane dirt road. Without warning, he heard a loud bang. He was pushed hard—jolted to the side. Blackness came quickly into his view. That was all he remembered.

He woke with a start, finding himself sitting on a large rock next to a beautiful deep blue rushing river. The air seemed to smell so clean. He looked around and saw that the trees behind him across the blue sparkling river were lush, green, and tall—just perfect.

"Where am I?" he said to himself.

"You like the view?" an adult and familiar sounding male voice asked, standing in front of him in the near distance.

Matt had to squint his eyes at first and focus more. It was then he saw the male figure.

"Dad?" Matt was shocked. He felt chills run down his spine. Was it excitement or panic? He just couldn't believe who he was actually seeing.

His father, Joseph, had died several years back from a car accident, and here his dad was, in plain sight. He looked younger than the age he was when he died. His dad was vibrant looking again. Matt also noticed there was some type of light—was it around his dad or was it emanating through him? Matt wasn't really sure.

"Dad, is it you for sure? How can this be?" He raised a hand to cover his eyes from the sunlight. Or was it sunlight?

"Oh, it's me all right. Like the way I look?" His dad smiled, taking in the sight of his son. That beaming smile immediately calmed Matt down.

"You see now what prayers said for me can do?" his father said to Matt, turning easily and slowly around. His dad wanted Matt to fully see his spirit dressed in garments of glowing soft white with interpenetrating small shimmers of emerald green. It looked like his dad had on a casual overshirt with comfortable dress pants. Matt couldn't tell for sure, because dad's garments were gently rippling back and forth.

"I'm so happy to see you! You look amazing!" Matt exclaimed, then got up and rushed to hug his dad who was also happy to oblige. Matt could catch a whiff of a soft fragrance.

Was that coming from his father or somewhere else? Before he could ask his dad, a flash of memories showed themselves in his mind, like on a movie screen. Matt paused for a moment.

He remembered how fond he and his dad were of each other when dad was alive. It was a bond of love and trust that was not broken. He flashed on nature walks, baseball, mystery, and action movies they shared. He also recalled dad's pride concerning Matt's college graduation. He also recalled some of the arguments, too. Although not many, some of them were doozies.

Matt felt like it was as if his dad never left, except of course, for how he looked now, not like his bruised and broken physical body lying lifeless in the car when dad died. The doctors said it was better that his dad had died instantly, because he felt no pain. Otherwise, his dad could have greatly suffered.

"Hey, Joe, where am I? Is this a dream?" Matt asked, his thoughts gliding back into the timeless moment. Matt used to lovingly tease his father, calling him by his first name. People in the family used to remark how much the two of them seemed so much alike.

"Son, you're sort of in a dream, and sort of not." Joe said, giving Matt a wink after they separated from their greeting embrace.

"Oh, that's nice and clear as mud!" Matt quipped back with humor, realizing also that he, himself, was feeling so much better. The stress, tension, and desire for a swig of scotch whiskey vanished into thin air.

Matt was as calm, carefree and peaceful as could be. He breathed in deeply, taking in the amazing fresh air and stretched his body like he did before taking a walk or exercising.

"Dad, I have such a wonderful feeling. This place is so beautiful. Where is it? Come on, tell me, where am I?" Matt asked, looking around while waiting in anticipation for the answer.

"Matt, you're in an in-between place. It all is presenting itself to you in a dream-like state. That way you don't get yourself worked up because it's a state within yourself that you can accept." Joe became quiet waiting for some type of response.

"Dad, you've got to be kidding me!"

"No, I'm not son. God allowed me to come here to be with you. I'm always watching over when I can. It's true, love does not die, and life does go on beyond the grave." Joe paused. He really wasn't sure what Matt's response would be. It was one thing to believe in all of this, but another to experience one's soul leaving the body—whether it be temporary or not.

"Uh … am I … dead?" Matt asked the question slowly, not very certain he wanted to hear the answer.

"Actually, yes … and … no." Joe chuckled, knowing his son wasn't going to take that for an answer.

"Joe, can you be a little clearer? It was always one way or the other with you, not this in- between yes and no stuff. What happened since you crossed over? Did you get soft around the edges?" Matt felt an inexplicable inward joy that was hard to contain. He was so grateful to be able to see his dad again and to joke with him.

"Ha…ha…very funny," his father answered back with playful sarcasm.

Joe put his arm around Matt's shoulder. "Let's take a little stroll alongside this river."

Matt and his dad leisurely walked alongside the rushing clear blue water. They were headed toward what seemed to be a beautiful setting sun. The weather was perfect, and the temperature was warm, but not hot. A gentle breeze was blowing.

"You're preparing for a choice you know, and I'll make this quick, because I can't stay long." Joe said.

Matt's dad grew more urgent. He knew that even though time did not exist where he was, it did for Matt with his physical body still on earth.

"That choice is whether you want to go up there," his dad said and looked up giving the indication of heaven. "Or, whether you want to stay on earth. So, it's a choice of either wanting to live or to die."

"Where did this come from?" Matt was completely taken aback, not only with what was being said, but how plain, simple and straight forward it was delivered by his father.

"It came from Above, my son. I told you God gave me permission to speak with you. That's the only way I've been allowed to be here. Joe looked straight toward the setting sun and continued. "By the way, your mom loves you and says hello. She looks great! We're dancing again. She'd be here, but I was the one, at the moment, meant to come see you."

His dad gave him a wide smile and with his copper-colored eyes shining, he gave his son another wink.

"Dad, I think about you and Mom a lot. Give her a big hug for me."

Matt could feel a tear of joy trickle down his cheek, not just believing, but knowing both of his parents were happy.

With everything he was experiencing here, along with his own father's presence, Matt began to realize he didn't want to go back. He didn't want to face any more issues and arguments on earth.

"Dad, I want to stay here with you and Mom. I've done the best I can, and I've loved my wife, but I don't want the problems there. And besides, I don't think Melissa loves me anymore anyway."

"Matt, it's not that simple. There is more to know about staying here and how to get to heaven—more than you may know right now.

Yes, the choice is yours. However, first ask yourself this question. Do you honestly think Melissa doesn't love you?" Waiting for his reply, Matt's Dad fell silent and just looked down at the beautiful ivory-colored sand beneath him.

"What happened to me, Dad?"

"Well, you were in a car accident, another reason why I'm here," his dad answered.

"It can't be! I was just backing out of the parking area by the lake. I looked in the rear-view mirror. I was backing out slowly!" Matt exclaimed.

"Oh, yes, it can be … and it was … a car accident. Nasty one, too," his father said.

"Tell me more because I don't remember much of anything…" The sound of Matt's voice trailed off, as he tried to recall what had occurred.

"Some rebellious teenagers cut school and went for a joy ride. They also decided to hide a bottle of vodka and some limewater in the car. They drove to the lake, and thought no one was around, so they gunned it. You couldn't see it coming. They were speeding and hit you hard enough on that passenger's side to knock you out. You banged your head. The impact also banged up your body some, too. Son, don't get upset, but your vehicle is a mess!"

By the way his dad said it, they both couldn't help but start chuckling out loud about the vehicle being a mess. The laughing between them calmed Matt's bewilderment about his own accident.

Suddenly, a different sensation came rushing in. It was a deep feeling of love mixed with such sadness, that it flooded Matt's spirit. Then, that feeling brought up an image, a scene in front of his eyes. It was of his wife, Melissa. She was crying. He could feel in his heart how much Melissa did love him. Yet, Matt also saw that there he stood with another drink in his hand, as he rationalized away what he was doing.

The next scene flashed in his mind. It was of his dad's car. His dad rarely drank, but when he did, he "tied one on" as he would say. His dad did drink that night and drove when he shouldn't have. He missed the bend in the road. The rest, Matt didn't want to see anymore.

"Stop these scenes… these visions!"

They didn't stop. The next was the most recent. It was Matt's own accident. He saw him talking to himself and drinking from the flask. In a flash, he was shown that the driver who hit him was also drinking behind the wheel.

"Dad, make it stop!" Matt cried out, feeling the embarrassment and the anguish of recognizing the truth much more than he wanted to admit. Matt was drinking and not paying attention. The teenagers that hit him were drinking too. This car accident and his wife wanting to leave were hard lessons to swallow, let alone needing to admit his own mistakes.

"How do you want to live your life, son? Is this the road you want to take? Is this the choice?" Joe cradled Matt in a warm hug of affection, as the questions posed caused anguished realizations for his beloved son who stopped short and couldn't walk any farther.

His dad released the embrace and continued talking. "If I had to choose it over again my son, I wouldn't have had any drinks that night. Sure, I didn't drink much at all, so I said to myself. It's okay to tie one on, because I don't do it—hardly at all. I rationalized, son. Are you?"

His dad's loving and calm voice kept repeating the same question, trailing off as his image slowly faded in the distance.

"Dad!" Matt shouted to him. "Don't go!"

Matt became frightened realizing what was happening to his own soul. He was going down the wrong road and couldn't see it. Melissa was right.

Right then, Matt knew he couldn't and didn't want to stay. He had to make things right again first.

"Forgive me!" he cried out standing there. It seemed Matt was calling to his dad, but he was really calling out to God, and he knew it.

The river, the setting sun, his father—it all faded.

"Forgive me." Then blackness took over—again—for a while.

Matt faintly heard another voice, one that was unfamiliar. She seemed to be asking him to wake up. He felt her hand gently jostle his shoulder. Her voice called to him. The sound woke him up. He took a deep, languid breath and groggily tried to open his eyes. He could do it, but not all the way. Both eyes were swollen almost completely shut.

Matt tried to rise to a sitting position but couldn't raise himself all the way up. He felt like a lead weight had knocked him on the head and boy did it hurt. All he could barely do was try. He could feel the pain and heaviness of his body. He knew all too well that he was back.

"My father was right, I have to stop drinking," he thought.

Matt was still groggy, but alert enough to feel the throbbing physical headache. He touched the side of his head with his free hand and felt the bandages.

He slowly looked down again and noticed that his left arm was in a full cast cradled by a sling up to his elbow. Matt also saw that his left calf, down to his toes, was covered in a hard, white cast. He felt like his whole body was a heavy, weighted down form, throbbing and burning with pain.

"I think I need some medicine. No, I know I need something

for pain," Matt whispered, trying to get up so the nurse would hear. It was hard to do. His headache hurt.

"Whoa! Settle down my young man," came the voice of a kind-faced, mature woman. She was the head nurse on the floor where he was staying.

"You're going to be all right, thank goodness. However, you have to lie back down, and I'll be back with your pain meds," she said, giving him a wink that seemed so much like his father's.

The nurse helped lay him back down, re-adjusted his head pillow and left the room.

Melissa, having been seated in a corner away from the hospital bed, didn't know he was awake. She was distraught and softly crying, her head bowed in prayer.

"Sweetheart," Matt called to her with a soft, soothing tone.

Startled and happy all at once, Melissa got up and rushed to his bedside.

"Oh Matt, I'm so sorry this happened." She responded tenderly and leaned in close to his face. Their lips pressed together in a long, gentle kiss.

Matt tenderly took in the entire slender and willowy frame of his loving wife. He also noticed that Melissa's dark auburn hair was pulled back into a low-looped type bun with strands hanging loose at the base of her neck. In her eyes, there he saw the signs of relief mixed with joy. Tears trickled down her cheeks.

Knowing Melissa still loved him was like having an invisible, sweet healing balm for his soul. He realized how lucky he was.

"I thought I'd lost you," Melissa said.

Matt deeply felt the love he had for his wife and knew it was her voice he heard in that in-between place. He realized that is what pulled him back into his body.

"I love you Melissa, and I'm so sorry. Don't leave me. You were right. I'm heading down the wrong road. I don't want to. I need help to stop drinking."

Taking the wedding ring from her pocket, she placed it back on Matt's finger. The gold band caught the light from the window. Its color glistened.

The wedding ring and the ivory-colored rosary she gave him were the only two items pulled from the wreckage.

"I won't leave you. I love you," Melissa quietly responded, as she touched the gold band on his finger.

The flask of whiskey in Matt's Jeep Wrangler was never found.

"Blessed is the influence of one true,
loving human soul on another."
—GEORGE ELIOT

Lion and the Lamb

A SLENDER LOOKING young woman stood up from resting against a tree stump, dusted herself off, and started walking again. Her strawberry blonde, shoulder-length hair moved softly with the breeze.

She enjoyed strolling the winding horse trail. It was cut right in the middle of an emerald haven of plush, green forest with hills, valleys and a wide, rushing river.

Even though her real name was Casey Dawson, her friends and family called her Kip. It started in grade school when one of her friends just started calling her by that name. The only explanation about it was that she looked like a "Kip." She liked it and kept the nickname ever since.

Her friends, even more than her own family, knew she had strong intuition. When necessary, she could be very insightful—even into the invisible world beyond this natural one.

The wind felt warm, gentle and caressing as she walked one of the winding Vancouver trails. The path led down a small hill and back again to flatter ground. It was there she noticed the two wide, plush green trees, one on either side of her. Suddenly, she felt like she was pushed back gently, as if an invisible force wanted her to stop for a moment, to be still—and look.

Kip could sense there was no danger, just a soft beckoning inside her to look around.

Before she could understand what happened, the whole area around her and as far as she could see, shifted in energy. It seemed to have changed into what looked like an enchanted forest, like the one a child reads about in fairy tales.

"What's going on here?" she thoughtfully questioned, attuning to the change.

It was as if Kip was taken out of time and placed at the entrance of a special area. She could smell the wonderful fragrance of lilacs, and the fresh scent of green grass—all the while breathing in what seemed to be such clean, pure air. She looked down the half sunlit forest path. Noticing the river along the right side of the trail, Kip had never seen such deep blue in any waters she had known. It was truly a beautiful, magical place.

"It's the wind again," Kip mused while she was gently nudged to walk down the hill, being encouraged to move along. As she did, something inside her changed as well.

Kip seemed to understand what the animals and birds were communicating. In an unusual way, she thought she could hear the plants, flowers, and even some trees communicating, too.

"No, this can't really be," she said to herself. "It's just me." Yet again, she saw the same chipmunk scurry past her communicating in its way, the same thing.

It was then she realized it was true. This forest was special, and she felt as if all in this forest were her relations in some way.

Kip thought back to the lessons she had learned from some very special Native American elders. She recalled their telling her to be more connected with the land and nature relations. Back then, they also told her that a moment would come when she would truly understand what it means to respect all life, for all are brothers and sisters. Kip knew in her heart that this was that moment.

She continued walking the beautiful and transformed trail. On either side, the trees seemed to wave hello, various birds—small and large—chirped or shrieked an acknowledgment. She glanced to her right when she heard the sound of the rushing river. She noticed how sparkling blue the water was and how it combined with the white tips of the small waves splashing. Her senses were invigorated and refreshed. What amazed Kip most were all the colors.

"Heavenly!" she thought.

Slowly strolling along the path, she noticed how striking every color was—nothing like she sees in ordinary time. The green and red hues of the leaves and flowers she saw came alive with radiance. The various hues of blue, purple and white blended so beautifully with one another, she wondered if an angel was instructed by God to paint on the canvas of this forest. The verdant green grass was rich looking, and the gold of the sun's rays seemed divinely inviting—so warm, but not hot. To Kip, it was all just breathtaking.

She stopped for a moment, bent down toward the ground and picked up some of the rich, dark brown soil. Even though the ground was solid and sure, it still felt like thick velvet.

"This is amazing!" she said out loud, as she brushed the dirt from her hands and stood back up to continue walking. "I feel so privileged to have this experience!"

She looked up and saw the clear aquamarine blue sky. The floating clouds were soft, puffy and white—so stunning, that it was actually unexplainable.

As she took her time and tried to soak in the experience, a special verse told to her by a medicine woman teacher came quickly to her mind.

"There is beauty above me, beauty below me, beauty in front of me, beauty behind me. There is beauty all around me," she murmured softly. A profound feeling of joy mixed with gratitude swelled within her.

Just then, that sound—that distant roaring echo stopped her dead in her tracks. Inexplicable feelings of joy suddenly turned into eerie apprehension. She knew that sound, who wouldn't. It was the distant roar of a lion. Her heart began to race.

"Did I really hear that sound? What do I do?" Kip asked herself these scrambled questions, quickly trying to assess the situation. She didn't dare move forward, for she didn't know what she would face, let alone be able to defend herself against a lion. All she had was a bowie knife. It would not be enough against a male lion, not unless Kip was close enough to him. Even then, she knew she would only have one slim chance.

"I'm just imagining this," Kip tried to steady her nerves and rationalize her instinct.

The impression hit her again. It was a male lion in the distance, but gaining on her scent, nonetheless. She just knew it.

"No! no, this can't be happening!" Her feelings of apprehension crashed into a pool of panic and fear. Kip froze for a moment—right there on the spot.

For a split second, she couldn't move.

"I can't do this to myself. I have to think."

With a deep breath, she temporarily shook herself loose from the fear and scrambled up the large grassy and wooded knoll. She was looking for a place to hide.

Kip found a crater-size dirt hole created from a partially uprooted sequoia tree. Her body was small enough to fit. There was no other place to go. So, she jumped down—right into it. Then, Kip braced herself against the back dirt wall.

"It's not big enough for a lion," Kip thought to herself.

This hole was the only spot. Although cornered, she knew at least here, she might have a chance. Kip wanted to wait it out and call for help.

"Why is this happening to me?" Kip's thoughts raced. "I don't understand any of this." She was shaking and tried to breathe slowly to calm down. She needed to keep her wits about her. The sound of that roar was much closer.

Kip quieted herself and stayed as still as possible. This was the only way she might survive. Beads of sweat began to form on her bronze, tanned skin.

Suddenly, the lion, with its muscular strength, lurched at her outside that cave-like hole then backed off.

"Get back!" Kip shouted, gasping at the sight.

The sound of this lion's roar was so forceful, it raised a cloud of dust from the ground. It caused her to jerk back against the dirt wall. Her shoulder blades and muscles ached from having slammed back.

"Help, Help!" Kip screamed and quickly grabbed the handle of the knife still secured in the brown-beaded pouch specially made. It was fastened to the left side of her belt. She gripped that knife handle so hard, her hand trembled from the fisted hold.

She could only see a side partial view of his head and body. Kip could tell it actually was a mature male lion. Her intuition had been correct.

This fierce-looking animal bore a thick, shaggy mane covering the backside of his head and shoulders. The cascading of light-to-dark colored hairs were both a magnificent, yet frightening sight.

As the lion turned to face that cave opening, Kip saw that his head was massive. His intense, predator stare could have conveyed a deadly warning. Instead, this slow-breathing lion just stared down at her and didn't move.

"Massive and magnificent!" Kip murmured in awe. She could tell that this lion was every bit of 500 pounds. Although she was scared for her life, she couldn't help but admire this strong and beautiful creature.

At the moment she spoke those words, the lion, instead of roaring again, gave a low growl sound that came out like quiet rolling thunder. It was as if he heard and understood what she had said.

"Help me, someone, please!" Kip yelled out again, trying to be bold and loud in an attempt to also shoo the lion away.

"Get out! Get away!" Kip commanded forcefully.

As soon as those words left her lips, the lion lurched forward again, sweeping his large forepaw at her fast and hard. Kip's eyes widened, as she slammed back against the dirt wall again. It was one swipe and the lion stopped, as if only to warn her.

Warning enough it truly was, for she knew those forepaws could badly wound or even kill her. Kip fell silent, breathing hard.

"Come out," Kip heard. The lion's words were plain as day. Yet, there was no human sound. The lion spoke to her in a way she could somehow understand. Kip was really scared. She had to try gathering courage.

"No!" she said firmly. She had to remind herself to breathe more slowly—to try and calm her racing heart and mind. She didn't release the hold on her knife.

"Come out. I won't hurt you," the lion called out again in a calm, low growl sound.

"No way! I'm not coming out. I would have to have a death wish to do that. You'll kill me, then eat me." Kip spoke emphatically in a loud voice.

She was trying to hide the trembling and fear, but she knew it wasn't working. Her mature attempt at courage melted into sounding a bit more comical than emphatic and strong.

"I don't trust you. Why are you here anyway? Why am I here with you?" Kip questioned firmly.

"I said I won't hurt you. You've seen me before," the lion responded.

"What?" Kip called back in total surprise.

Then there was silence between both of them. She thought a moment and suddenly, as if it had been placed there in her mind, she recalled a dream she had before. She was in a meadow and saw a male lion, just like him, standing next to her more as a friend and protector rather than a predator.

"No, it couldn't be," she called out to him. "This is just a deception, something to lure me out."

She could see him shake his head as if to say, "No." Then she saw this lion drop its muscular, compact body slowly and easily to the ground—as if relaxing.

Kip could plainly see the lion wasn't going anywhere. At that moment she knew, neither was she.

She felt dizzy, and then darkness came into view.

When she opened her eyes, Kip hadn't initially realized that she had fainted. From the tension, the fear, the cramped dirt space—all of it had caused her to pass out. She wasn't sure just how long she had been unconscious.

"Darn it!" Still feeling unsteady, Kip tried to make a phone call but couldn't get a connection. She slid the mobile phone back into the rear pocket of her jeans.

Kip had to get out of this cramped, dirt dungeon and somehow get back to where she was. She looked up and out the opening. The lion was gone.

"Should I try to get out now?" she wondered. "Yes!" she affirmed back to herself.

Kip quickly reached up and grabbed a thick, long root just at the rim of the opening. She cautiously began pulling herself up.

Just as she was near the top, she saw the lion. He had something white in his mouth. It was the body of a live animal, but Kip couldn't tell at first exactly what kind of animal it was.

"Lord, help me!" She called out, as the lion rushed toward her.

She screamed, fell back down and slammed against the back dirt wall yet another time. Kip could feel the increasing pain in her back shoulder muscles, at the same time she heard a "baa" like calling. It was a soft, gentle sound.

She realized the lion had a lamb in his mouth and had dropped it gently on the rim of the opening. He had not harmed the lamb in any way but had carried it to her.

Kip let go of the handle of the knife, and as fast as she could, she grabbed the lamb and pulled it into that small dirt cave with her. She was certain she wanted to take that chance in order to keep it safe from harm. Kip could tell it was a young, male lamb.

Holding the lamb gave her comfort in the tense situation realizing that at least he was safe from the lion's jaws. She, too, somehow felt safe by nestling him in her arms and feeling the soft and thick, crimped white and beige-colored hairs. Kip noticed this lamb did not have any horns.

"The lamb was walking. I followed him. I told him about you. He wanted me to carry him to you. I have," the lion communicated.

"Then why did you roar, growl and swipe at me?" She firmly demanded.

"You needed to be silenced long enough for me to speak. If I hadn't caused such a distraction, I know, and so do you, that you would have continued to loudly try to shoo me away. As if you could," the lion retorted almost as if smiling at his own comment.

"I've been aware of you for a while, Kip, and I know that once you are determined enough, you will just keep right at it, won't you?"

Kip stopped talking long enough to hear, or thought she could hear the lamb speak, too.

"Yes, Kip, you can hear me as well," the lamb communicated through the gentle baaing sounds. "And lion is right," the lamb said in agreement.

Kip released the lamb's small body onto the dirt ground just next to her. Neither could move much. It was so tight a fit in that dirt enclosure.

She began to cry softly from the frustration, knowing they were both right, and because she was hearing animals talk. To make matters worse, she was trapped in a tree-rooted dirt space.

One thing Kip could never handle easily at all, was being constrained, held down or restricted in any way. Yet, it was even more than that.

Just days ago, she was frustrated and deeply upset. The argument occurred between herself and someone close to her. Kip felt he just kept talking, being angry and wouldn't listen—that he just kept going on and on. Both were stubborn, as usual. She felt trapped. He left. She cried and felt she had no peace within her.

Remembering, Kip came to realize that she too, was caught in the trap of angrily fighting back with her words and being stubborn.

"Yeah, well, in general, you both may be right. You've got to admit though, that this, right here now, is no ordinary situation, and I'm not coming out!" Kip said boldly calling out to the lion.

"I've got plenty of time. I'll just stretch out here and wait. It's relaxing." Lion lazily low- growled the words, knowing that the way those words were said and her being stuck in the circumstances, would all start to incite her to action. Lion also knew the lamb wanted her to come out.

"Well, I'll be!" Kip snapped back, her fear lessening and determination beginning to set in. Here she was, feeling trapped—again. She was hardly able to move. Just above her on the flat, open ground was a massive lion talking to her, not knowing if he really would harm her or not. Next to her in this dirt hole and without much room to move, was a young, male lamb who was talking to her, too.

Kip's hand ached from the tension of clutching the knife handle. Kip also hadn't noticed the red, raw scrapes under her forearms. Underneath her blue jeans riding across the shins of both legs were also raw scrapes from jumping into the large hole in the first place. She didn't feel the pain until she shifted her position and felt her jeans rub up against the abrasions.

"Ow, ow!" Kip blurted out in pain. She bent over trying to look at her shins. That action brought the shoulder and muscle pain to bear as well.

"That did it. I've had enough!" Kip called out in anger, pointing her index finger up at the lion.

"Lion, how dare you try to tell me how I act, as if it is my fault for all of this. It was you who chased down my scent and wouldn't let it go. It was you roaring so loud you created dust from the dirt, and it was you who took a swipe at me with your forepaw!" Kip shouted, the adrenaline rushing up within her.

Blind courage she didn't think she had, feeling trapped, and the raw scrapes causing pain is what moved her to action.

Kip grabbed a sturdy root and again pulled her way up. This time she climbed up and out of that dirt dwelling.

She was sweating and unsteady. Quickly she regained her balance, and with that smell of fresh air mixed with dirt aroma, she also came to her senses.

"Oh, what…have…I… done?" Kip gasped. The shocking awareness of what she had just done riveted through her. She was now near this powerfully built, 500 pounds of animal power.

One minute she saw him stretched out on the grassy knoll. The next minute he was standing—dead center—facing her. The action was so fast, Kip could hardly believe it. She stumbled backward over a rock but caught herself, her hand positioned back on the knife.

Lion stood there, steady and still. She saw him face her, his golden-colored eyes piercing and intent, as he stared at her. To Kip, his pupils looked larger than life at that moment, and so did he.

Both held their positions. Kip was stunned at what she had just done and inwardly anguished for something to think, to say, to do.

"Should I move, strike, or stay still?" Her thoughts raced for an answer, as her hands trembled, keeping them both locked together now, as one, on that bowie knife.

"Yes, you've done it, and if I were you, I'd stay still," came the lion's answer.

"You used your anger to gain courage and to say you've had enough of feeling downtrodden in whatever way that has been for you. You've stood your ground. However, in all the quick questions you posed in your mind, striking would not have been the right thing to do," the lion, now calm again, explained.

Lion relaxed his firm stance, took a step forward and continued. "Blind courage mixed with anger instead of inner strength and control has its definite and deep pitfalls."

This strong, large animal slowly moved closer and stopped.

"Did you not sense, know deep within that I could have ripped that hole apart with a few swipes of my paws, making a wider opening? If you were simply prey, we wouldn't be here this long already," the lion explained further.

Lion eased closer still. Now he stood before Kip. Seeing him up close like this, she felt dumbstruck. Her body tensed. She widened her stance to keep balance. The width of his head, strong body and powerful forelegs utterly amazed her. She had never been around a lion in any way.

"I...I...don't...I don't know what to say." Kip stuttered, so in awe of this animal's presence and wisdom.

"I also carried the lamb to you without harming it. You also sensed you knew me as a protector, a guardian of sorts did you not?" Lion conveyed with more gentleness now.

Yes, Kip did sense the lion really wouldn't harm her. She also recalled the dreams and wondered why he hadn't pawed away the loose dirt, because the ground wasn't rock hard.

For a flash of a second, in between fear and survival, she also wondered why a lion would bring a lamb in its mouth and place it gently at the opening of that cave-like hole.

"All of that I did sense, see and know," Kip said more softly, settling down. "My disbelief shoved it away." The inner tug of a sorrowful sigh came next.

"This would be hard to believe for anyone! Is this a dream or a test?" Confusion mounted, as Kip pushed back the tangled, sweat-filled bangs from her forehead.

"A test...a dream...maybe both." Lion answered as he circled her slowly, staring intently at her.

"You are not at peace either," Lion said, circling back around to face her and continue. "You're still struggling as are so many in the natural world; grappling to believe and accept that peace can and will occur someday." Lion's words and low steady breathing were soothing to Kip.

"I so hope for that, but it is so hard to really believe." Kip could feel her tension slowly, gently flushing away. She relaxed her defensive stance and took both hands away from her knife.

"Yes, it is hard to believe because of the current state most see— strife, war, famine— cruelty to one another. There are pockets of good will, peace, and kindness. You and the rest of humanity get real glimpses, but there is not yet a burning flame of believing," the lion said in the soft low-growl tone Kip was getting used to.

Lion moved forward and slightly past her. Curving his head back toward her, the lion said, "Yet I tell you that peace and the Good Shepherd are coming. One day all will know. Kip, you will see a sign which will show you that what has been said will be so…one day it surely will."

Kip wanted so much to receive this confirmation, because she did hope for it so much in her own heart.

"I'm sorry," Kip said in apology, wiping away trickled tears from her cheek.

Shedding her fear, Kip approached the lion. She stroked his mane and laid her head against his thick fur. It was like a thick, coarse, yet comforting pillow. She knew he would instinctively understand the sincere gesture.

Lion closed his eyes in caring acceptance, as he nuzzled her slightly with the side of his head.

"You needn't worry. I came at first to test you. How much courage might you have? You have shown me that you have courage enough." Lion was gentle with his words.

"Thank you for the test and helping me understand more." Kip released her embrace and took a few steps back.

Lamb came up easily out of that dirt cave and darted toward her, then gently nudged her with his nose.

"I almost forgot you were there," Kip warmly smiled, bending down quickly to give the lamb a heartfelt hug. There was something about this young lamb she couldn't put her finger on exactly. His wool shown with a soft brilliance that was so comforting, she couldn't explain it. She just felt filled with peace.

"Is this just all a dream?" she silently thought.

"In what you consider is a dream, there is a message we both would like you to take and share. That is why I have come," Lion said to her having sensed her thoughts.

"Lion, who are you?" Kip interrupted him. "I have to know." She waited patiently.

"You remember the story. It is in the book of Daniel. He was not harmed, for I laid down and closed my mouth upon the angel's command."

Kip was completely taken aback. "I don't know if I can handle this…" Her words, having trailed off, sounded like a whisper.

"Do not be afraid. Just know and share with those who will hear. There shall come a day…" Lion abruptly stopped from communicating anymore.

Truly in awe, Kip literally could not speak, because the lion and the lamb both vanished in a burst of shining white glow. Kip shielded her vision by closing her eyes because of the vibrant light.

When Kip opened her eyes again, she found herself sitting on the ground as she was— before all this happened. Her back was up against the tree stump.

"Was I asleep?" she said to herself. "I'm at the tree stump where I first sat down."

She looked around, and farther down the trail, she could see those same two green plush trees.

"I must have dozed off. It was all a dream, but what a powerful experience, that's for sure!" Kip told herself as she automatically reached for her scarf, but it wasn't there.

"Hmm…where is it? Oh well, I can't think about that right now."

Kip stood up, stretched away the stiffness but felt some pain at the back of her shoulders. She didn't pay any attention to it and dusted herself off from the ground's grassy debris.

Curious, she decided to walk down that hill again toward those two green trees. That's when she noticed it. The soft ivory cotton scarf she loosely wore around her neck was caught in one of the tree's branches.

"How could my scarf have gotten here; at the same place I saw myself walking in my dream?" She shook her head, explaining to herself that it might have blown off her neck with the wind while she was sleeping.

Noticing it was now dusk, Kip thought it best to turn around and head for her car. She wasn't used to walking a trail at this time of day. The soft yellow and deeper orange color of the warm, setting sun helped her feel more peaceful. It all reminded her of the western-saddle trail rides she took on her horse. She also felt a slight burning pain on her shin underneath her pant leg and avoided dealing with it until she was back at home.

Kip got into her car and rolled down the window for more of that fresh country air. She turned the ignition key and just let the motor run a while. Kip sat there quietly going over in her mind what had happened. While reviewing the message entrusted to her to give to others, she kept wondering.

"Was it a dream? It had to be, wasn't it?" Kip went back and forth, questioning herself. Whatever it was, she knew it was the most powerful experience she had encountered.

"Don't we all, deep down, want to feel peaceful—to be at peace?" she thought, as she buckled her seat belt.

Kip was driving down the road when she heard a breaking news story come across the radio. The city zoo had two animals escape—a lion and a young, male lamb. Bolts had come loose on each cage during the long truck transit to Vancouver. While being unloaded, the cage doors of both animals were easily opened with some shoves from each creature. The easiest and most obvious was from the lion first. This is what caused the escape incident.

"Both these animals seem like they're running almost side-by-side! The lion isn't trying to attack the lamb!" said the on-scene radio reporter whose tremulous voice caused Kip to turn up the radio.

"This is…wait a minute," the radio announcer paused. Kip could hear him breathing hard, as if he were running closer to where, she didn't know yet.

"There they are! I see them ahead of some trees. They both just stopped and are starting to lie down on the grass in the large community park!" The reporter's excited voice switched to sounding softer while trying to catch his breath.

"I can't believe this is happening right here in our community park! Both lion and lamb have laid down, side-by-side!" The on-location reporter just could not contain his emotions.

On the radio, Kip could also hear the hustle and bustle of sounds as people, and other reporters were gathering.

Kip pulled over to the side of the road and stopped the car. There it was, the sign. It was the sign of the times yet to come. It could not have been more obvious.

"Thank You," is all she could say, as tears trickled down her face.

"The wolf also shall dwell with the lamb, and the leopard shall lie down with the kid; and the calf and the young lion and the fatling together; and a little child shall lead them."
—ISAIAH 11:6.

Pebbles and Protection

AMBER CAME BACK to her small-town community in Washington County, Vermont. She had her fill of disappointment and sadness living the big city life elsewhere. She was hoping to gain some peace being back home.

Amber left church after attending early morning Sunday service. It was late spring. She could feel the warmth of the sun as she walked out of church and noticed there wasn't a dark cloud above. The sky was beautiful ocean blue and the slowly passing clouds puffy white.

"I'm going to walk," she thought, "and I know it will take a while, but I need the exercise."

She headed toward the large community woodland where one could walk or bike ride. There also was a large, spacious meadow of cleared trees.

Amber Stone was thirty-five-years old who stood at five feet, six inches. She was of medium build with a soft, warm tone to her skin. Her dark, waist length hair generally caught someone's attention.

Gentle strokes of bronze and soft smoky eye shadow enhanced her deep brown eyes which often expressed care and emotion.

Today, however, even though she had just left the comfort of the church service, Amber's sentiments again bubbled up raw from beneath the surface. Yes, today and for a long while now, Amber was feeling hurt and alone. She ached inside. It took a lot for her not to let it show, which was something not easy for her.

"Maybe I'll feel better once I get to my quiet place," she whispered to herself. At this point, she felt it was one of the only uplifting places she could go. The other was attending church service, but even then, there were many times she had to force herself to get there.

While walking, she pondered what the pastor had said about no one ever being alone, even if they are feeling alone, because our angels are always with us. Although Amber believed that to be true, she sure wasn't feeling it in her heart or soul at this moment. She just wished that for once, she could get some real and solid confirmation for herself.

"Just once, is it asking too much?" She looked up, talking out loud this time, hoping heaven could hear. Amber's voice echoed her frustration.

"Thank goodness, I can talk out loud. No one is around to think I'm outside my mind," she said to herself, looking around once again to be sure no one was following.

Amber had been going through a darker time in her life. It was discernible, even to herself, that she felt lonely and even skeptical. It wasn't normally like her.

She hurried to the woodland and the special area. It was a peaceful place of refuge, tucked away in a corner off the beaten path and hidden by some overbrush. She had found it some time ago. No one was ever there, at least not at any of the times she had gone.

The dimly sunlit, hidden path gave way to a green rolling meadow of grass that was speckled with blue, yellow, lavender, and white-colored wildflowers. As she drew in a deep breath of fragrant air, the fresh aromas livened Amber's senses. She felt better.

When Amber looked up, she saw some birds perched on branches near and above her. The chirping sounds perked up her lowered feelings.

She picked her spot in that wonderfully colored meadow and sat down. She slung her small backpack over her shoulder so she could retrieve her journal book, which she thought of as her diary. It was wood-covered and had deer skin colored-like swirls sweeping across the front. In it were several lined pages.

Amber snatched the pen from the side-zippered pocket and began writing.

"Dear Diary, why do people judge? There are things I'm trying to understand, and I just don't. Why do people who say they care really don't, unless I do exactly what they expect of me according to how they think it should be. I know I might be sorry for saying this, but sometimes I feel that animals and pets are better companions than people are. But then again, who am I to talk? I'm far from perfect myself." Amber stopped writing to think more. She shifted her sitting position for better comfort and went back to put pen to paper.

"I'm tired right now of keeping up the positive attitude, I just don't feel happy," she admitted in writing, feeling a few watery tears welling up in her eyes.

Abruptly, Amber stopped writing because a pebble had been tossed onto her page. It was a small, round, grey and blue stone.

"What is this?" Amber asked out loud.

She knew it didn't fall. She was already sitting on the ground and nowhere near any place where stones were. It definitely had been tossed.

Amber became suspicious, and a few tears that had spilled on to her page stopped. Her feelings changed into a slow, building fear.

"Who's there?" She called out while staying seated, slowly perusing the entire area. A still silence was the only response.

Amber turned her head to the left to glance again. When she did another stone, coming from the right, sailed through the air and plopped on to her page. She gasped.

"Stop it and show yourself!" she called out with a stern voice, hiding her fear. Glancing to her right at the familiar group of trees, Amber saw some of the leaves rustling. She thought she saw someone but wasn't sure.

"Who are you over there? Stop trying to frighten me," she now demanded, rising quickly to her feet and ready to run out of the meadow if need be.

Just then, she saw an image of a man standing behind the trees. She couldn't see him fully due to the thick leaves that had shadowed the sunlight. She could tell, however, that he was motioning urgently for her to move away from where she was sitting.

"You'll be safer over here," the man's voice called to her. "I won't hurt you. I'm here to help."

For some strange reason, Amber felt drawn to the sound of his soft-spoken voice. Her trustworthy instincts revealed she could believe him, so she quickly moved from the spot and headed toward the voice.

As this man stepped forward from a small group of maple trees, Amber's breath caught in her throat when she saw his handsome chiseled features and how tall he stood. His eyes—crystalline blue and beaming with glistening light—is what captivated her soul. She could feel the invisible, spiritual power he exuded.

She stood there in his presence, his kind, yet intense gaze penetrated right through her. "Who...are...you?" Amber had trouble asking the question because she felt herself suddenly swoon. She thought she was going to faint.

"Do not be afraid," The man softly commanded. He quickly took her hand so she wouldn't fall.

Holding his hand, Amber instantly regained her balance and composure. She noticed the wind had whipped up and had caught several strands of his wavy brown hair, fluttering them against his forehead.

"Please tell me who you are," Amber said, urgently wanting him to reveal his identity.

"For now, just call me John."

Amber couldn't get a handle on the mixture of feelings she was experiencing. She only knew a part of her wanted to run because she wasn't sure of him even though he said not to be afraid. The other part of her felt peaceful, and soulfully soothed in his presence. Amber didn't know what to do.

Danger made her mind up for her.

"Get back!" John suddenly warned.

Amber heard voices—men's voices shouting, "Get the dog, get the dog! Don't let her run away!"

She spun around to see what was happening. What she heard first was panting, then the deep low threatening growl of a dog.

Amber squelched the terror rising within her, and without moving an inch, she slowly looked down. Just a few feet from her, she could plainly see the white, foamy froth dripping from the sides of the animal's curled up lips and bared teeth. She knew this dog. It was the curly-coated retriever she used to stop and pet on her way to church.

Zak, the ten-year-old boy, was screaming for the police not to shoot his pet. As Amber heard his desperate pleas, she also noticed the dog's black-furred body was covered in sweat.

It was obvious the animal was rabid. A part of her felt so bad for the dog and Zak, yet the other part of Amber felt frozen in fear.

"Oh! No….no!" Amber could no longer keep silent. The terrified sound of her voice echoed through the meadow.

There was no time. Amber knew it. All she could do was turn sideways and cover the side of her face and head with her arm. Instinctively, she leaned toward John, trying to shield her own form.

The animal was snarling and snapping as it leapt up at her to attack. Just then, out of the corner of her eye, Amber thought she saw the arch of a large bird's white wing drape over her.

"Was that a bird? It was too large, wasn't it, or was it?" Amber's thoughts raced, as her confusion mounted, and her fear heightened. It was all she could bear to take in—the man John, the dog, and what she thought she saw.

Amber squeezed her eyes shut. She could feel her heart pounding.

"Please God, don't let the dog hurt me," she cried out loud while trying to shield herself.

Just that fast, silence found its way through the shouts and crying. That sudden quiet caused Amber to slowly open her eyes. The first thing she felt, then saw, was the rough bark of the tree she had been leaning against.

The man called John was gone.

"But I was leaning against him—wasn't I?" She silently questioned herself.

Amber turned back toward the open meadow. Less than two feet from her lying on its side on the ground was the rabid dog. It had been shot with a dart to heavily sedate it.

The slow and heavy sound of the dog's breath could be heard by

Amber and those nearby who watched in sad and stunned silence. The boy, Zak, was one of them.

Luke Wood, one of the police officers, ran up to her.

"Ma'am, are you alright?" he asked, touching her shoulder.

"I'm okay. The dog didn't bite me." It was difficult, but Amber forced herself to try and reply calmly, not wanting the small crowd and especially Zak, to see that she was still trembling.

"Ma'am, I'll tell you. I've never seen anything like that! It was a miracle you didn't get bit." Officer Luke was amazed and continued. "The dog leapt right up toward your neck. But it was as if—I don't know—something there, but not there. Whatever it was pushed the dog off at the same time I was able to take the shot to tranquilize it." Officer Luke looked truly perplexed.

Dan, Luke's police partner, was stooped low to the ground. "Nah, it was more like the dog jumped up and lost some balance in the process is all. That's what most likely happened," Dan said while wrapping the dog in blankets.

"I don't know, if you're right about that for sure," Luke responded, but decided to drop any further conversation. He simply helped lift the heavy, limp animal, so he and his partner could remove the sedated, rabid dog from the scene.

Obviously shaken, Amber could see her own hands still quivering. To calm down, she took some slow, relaxing breaths, as she walked away from the tree, still glancing around to try and find the man who called himself John.

He was gone and Amber couldn't help but silently wonder. "Was he my guardian angel? Or had I just imagined it?"

"Maybe Luke's police partner was right. The dog just lost his balance which caused me to be saved from the attack." Amber's thoughts were interrupted by Zak's approach.

"I'm sorry. My dog would not have normally done that. She's sick!" Zak Asher, the ten-year-old, curly red-headed boy came toward her, crying. One of the pant legs of his blue denim coveralls was loosely stuffed inside his hiking boot.

"My dog got attacked by a rabid raccoon. We didn't know. By the time we found the puncture wound, it was too late!" Zak was out of breath from running to her. He was also sniffling as he spoke, trying to hold back his emotions while continuing to explain. "I was told when I first got her that she had her rabies shots. The previous owner lied. I could tell he didn't like her and just wanted to get rid of her. So, I took the dog. I named her, 'Midnight,'" Zak said. He was sobbing now, aware of the fate that awaited his animal companion.

"Zak, I am so, so sorry about your dog."

Amber placed both hands on either side of his squared shoulders, expressing her sympathy as tears welled up again in her own eyes. She felt so badly for the emotional pain this young boy was feeling. She saw him nod his acceptance of her apology, but his gaze remained cast down toward the ground.

She knew he couldn't speak anymore. Amber felt him break away from her gentle embrace. She watched him run—as fast as he could—out of the meadow.

A few weeks had passed since the incident. Amber was sitting at the small wooden table she had on her patio outside. Her morning cup of coffee was nestled firmly in her hand, as she thought about what had happened.

She was surprised to notice that she was emotionally feeling better and better each day. Amber wasn't half as upset as she was before about feeling lonely and skeptical. A slow, but steady healing from emotional hurts and family squabbles had been taking place.

"I may never know for sure if it was an angel. I may not even be believed if I said anything, because nobody saw him but me." Amber sighed and brought the cup to her lips.

She took a long sip of the dark, aromatic brew and glanced at the backpack she placed in front of her.

"I think it's a good morning to do some more writing," she said to herself. Amber grabbed the backpack and started fishing through it to find her diary.

When she had scrolled through the pages, she saw a round, grey-blue pebble lying in the crease of the diary. There was a note written on one of her pages.

"Amber Stone, don't fear. You are not alone and haven't been since you were born." It ended with, "Your friend and angel, whom you call, John".

The penmanship was beautiful. It was like nothing she, at least, had ever seen. Beneath the pebble in the crease, lay a small, wispy white feather.

Amber raced to her bedroom. There in a large glass container were the several pebbles she had picked up and saved over time.

She took the pebble from the crease of the diary and compared it to the ones she saved.

They were all the same. Small, round, and beautiful grey-blue stones were all nestled in that jar.

Flashes of scenes from the past ran through her mind. Various incidents—ones of joy, sadness, near escapes from injury, loss or illness—is where and when she always found that particular looking pebble. Every single one of those times she felt drawn to pick it up and save that small round stone.

"Yes, when I was young, I did call my guardian angel, John…I did!" she exclaimed softly to herself.

She now knew that every time she had picked up one of those pebbles, it was a message that her guardian angel was close by.

"It's true! I'm not alone, and I've never been alone." Amber's joy was hard to contain, as she blew a kiss up to heaven.

"Now, where is that other jar with the money in it I've been saving? I'm going to surprise young Zak with a new puppy."

"For He shall give his angels charge over
you, to keep you in all your ways"
—PSALM 91:11

Rocks and Roll

"WHAT DO YOU mean that God can give you answers through nature? I mean, I can certainly try to understand that if I were out in the woods, but I'm here, right in the middle of downtown Cleveland, Ohio, on East 9th street, and you're telling me look to nature?" Craig sighed, lifting his head to look up at the overcast sky.

"Okay, You created her, You handle her," he joked.

Craig Deacon was a tall and well-dressed figure of a man in his late forties. His charcoal, thick hair was tailored-cut with some of the back hair slightly covering his pressed white shirt collar. During the work week, he wore classic style three-piece suits. Today was no different.

He had come to learn a lot about life, and how to treat other people. He learned early—the hard way. Time, experience and in the past, losing what he felt was the love of his life, taught him the bitter lesson. However, it was one that also helped him grow to understand more about relationships and people in general.

This understanding was used in his law career and made his work unique in its own way—not what one would normally expect.

"Listen, Craig, you've been having a hard time with this one, because it seems such a bad situation, and you know there is a whole lot of money involved. You don't know if everything will turn out right." Melody, his younger sister, tried to explain as quickly and efficiently as she could. The light was about to change, and they would need to walk faster— each needing to get back to their respective jobs.

The light changed. Craig started quickly walking across the street.

"Hey wait up! I'm not done explaining to you," Melody said, following just slightly behind and hanging on to her shirtwaist jacket. The wind at the corner of 9th could really whip up at times.

Melody was seven years younger than her brother. She had an optimistic, often idealistic view of life. She was a perfect fit for service and customer relations, which was part of her job.

Craig was much more the down-to-earth realist than his sister. He knew he had to be. Melody always seemed to have more of that faith that comes from somewhere inside, that no matter what, things will work out.

Melody believed God could send answers and help in various ways, if one only knew how to really pay attention in a good, discerning manner. Craig would often tease her about that, but secretly admired her strong belief.

Melody had short, wavy red hair with hazel eyes, and although Melody loved being out in nature, she didn't like just sitting there basking in the sun to get a tan. Craig, on the other hand, felt relaxed sitting on a patio chair positioned on concrete while rubbing suntan lotion on his skin and soaking up the rays. Melody, a spry and athletic five foot, four-inch enthusiast for life became too restless just sitting for long periods.

"Will you wait up," Melody called out.

"Can't sis, I'll be late. You walk a little faster to keep up with me this time," Craig called back to her, then decided to slow his pace and let her catch up.

"Okay, finish what you were saying," he said, giving his usual blue-eyed side glance toward Melody when they walked together.

"Look, just say a sincere prayer, ask for awareness and help in the matter, His Will be done." Melody touched Craig's arm to stop him for that special moment of explanation.

"That's it?" he asked, matching her gaze, but uncertain if he would do what she suggested.

"Yes, and…then…" Melody said, stressing the words and continued, "while you walk to your office, be patient and appreciate the good things you see along the way. The answer in nature will find you," she said, as assuredly as she could.

"Geeze! I'm gonna be late!" Melody said looking down at her green-banded wristwatch.

"My dear brother, you'll see that I'm right!" Melody laughed.

Once again, Melody's familiar blast of faithful and energetic enthusiasm bubbled out. Craig could feel it sweep over him. She was a walking energy of hope.

He leaned down to give her a quick peck on the cheek in appreciation.

"Okay, okay. I'll try it." Craig playfully shook his head and bore the smile he knew she wanted to see.

"I just hope the answer comes fast. I need it today," Craig called out, as he watched her walk away and waving good-bye.

As a self-employed attorney, Craig thought it would be better to have a location downtown, not far from the Justice Center or the courts. He had been in this downtown location for several years.

Craig looked at his watch. He had more time than he thought, about forty-five minutes. He convinced himself to do what Melody suggested, so he stopped inside an open doorway of one of the buildings on his way.

"Lord, please help me with this negotiation. It sure doesn't look like anything is going to change. Please help me with what to do. This divorce negotiation could get really ugly. Thanks for listening."

With a heavy sigh he stepped back onto the sidewalk. He knew that this was one of the hardest divorce negotiations he had ever encountered. Neither party wanted to budge—about anything. Each of them was like a rock, heavy-weighted and fixed.

Craig continued toward his office. He knew what was ahead of him and was not looking forward to any of it.

Catching some of the warmth of the summer sun, he started observing as his sister suggested. Just then above the city street he noticed a bird sitting perched on a telephone wire.

Even though robins were not uncommon, it made him curious as to why he was drawn to just that one.

"That's odd. There are birds flying around here all the time. Why was I so aware of this one?" He murmured to himself.

Craig looked up and noticed that this robin was looking down—directly at him. It then cocked its head as if eyeing the ground.

Craig followed the robin's glance to the sidewalk. That's when he saw it, near the curb. There were two large rocks positioned there by someone or something, so they would be directly off the sidewalk. They were only a few inches apart.

Between the rocks having burst upward, was a small group of brilliant, yellow-colored flowers with a darker center eye. There they were—flowers amid rocks.

"Hmm…this is interesting. I didn't see that before. Flowers and rocks." Craig thought a moment, letting his internal senses take over.

"Maybe there is a positive solution to this really messy situation. Could my little sister be right? We'll see," Craig said to himself.

He paused and looked at his leather-strap wristwatch. He straightened his tie, drew in a deep breath, and slowly let it out.

"Here we go. I hope the symbolism was right," Craig murmured to himself.

Craig arrived at his destination. He opened the office door and saw the couple sitting across from each other at the dark, cherry wood conference table. They were waiting for him.

Later that evening, Craig walked out of his office and outside into the warm, evening sunset and gentle breeze. It had been a long, battling day of negotiations.

Craig stood there for a while, watching the orange setting sun diminish, inch-by-inch into the distant horizon.

As arbitrating attorney for this case, he was finally able to get the couple to compromise. There would be no court battle.

"Thank you, I appreciate it." Craig whispered his short, but sincere prayer. He also realized by this experience that his sister was right.

Yes, it was a rock-hard day, but…it ended up rolling out to be a smooth and peaceful evening.

In a concrete world, there it was—the answer was given to him through a bird's gaze and a little piece of nature.

Craig pulled his mobile phone from his jacket pocket and began to dial his sister's number.

"In every walk with nature one receives
far more than he seeks."
—JOHN MUIR

Something in
the Air

"YOU CAN'T BE serious." Todd laughed, a wide grin coming across his tanned face. "You mean to tell me there are invisible helpers who can show up on a dime when you need help? Seems to me, with them being so busy, it could take a bit longer, or maybe not at all."

He winked at Becky with a side glance as he drove the pickup truck down the two-lane highway. It was a nice easy drive—straight ahead—with greenery and some rocky bluffs alongside the road.

Todd Kramer was a strapping and towering young man with green eyes and dusky brown hair. Becky, on the other hand, was only five feet, two and one-half-inches. Todd loved cuddling her smaller athletic frame in his arms.

He lived and worked in the city as a real estate agent but was a country boy at heart. His family moved from the farm life to the city when he was a teenager, but his appreciation of country living and open roads never left him.

Todd believed more in what he could see right there in front of him. What he just couldn't get a handle on was the afterlife—the invisible world. He just wasn't one hundred percent sure there would be anything else once his life was over.

"Look, I think I just saw a male spirit up there on that rocky ledge." Teasing, Todd slowed down and briefly pointed upward.

He knew that Becky, his girlfriend, who was a chestnut-haired, blue-eyed beauty would, at any chance she got, try to slip in a conversation about the afterlife. He knew she was hoping to be the one to put him on a true path of believing in heaven, helpers, and angels. Still, Todd was skeptical.

"Stop teasing me about all of this," Becky said, turning toward Todd and playfully tapped his muscled right arm with her hand. Her long, thick hair waved across her shoulders as the wind blew into the open window on the passenger's side of the truck.

"You're my girl, Chestnut!" he playfully quipped, calling Becky by the nickname he had for her because of the color of her hair.

Becky Cahill, at twenty-eight years old, had experienced quite a bit of traveling. She was a cowgirl at heart and straight out of Texas. Yet, she also liked adventure. She was a faithful believer in God, country, and the human heart.

Becky unlatched her seat belt and slid over from the passenger's side to sit closer to Todd just for a little while. She didn't see any cars coming or going on that sparsely driven highway. She didn't think it would be a problem.

"I'm glad you came to that last riding competition. It was really sweet of you to help cheer me on. I heard you yelling out your encouragement. That was so special to me. I'm livin' my dream and you're part of it." Becky snuggled closer.

She had a bachelor's degree in psychology, and a good creative background too, but her love of nature and especially horses had called to Becky's heartstrings. She blossomed in knowledge and experience concerning horses. Winning quite a bit of money and trophies barrel-race riding in different parts of the country helped her to feel successful—accomplished.

Becky and Todd, dressed in their favorite casual blue jeans and lightweight sweatshirts, were leisurely enjoying the drive through the outskirts of Houston. It was quality time they made sure to share.

"I don't think it's any coincidence either, that we met while riding horses. Also, is it a coincidence that you just happened to be in Texas visiting one of your friends who just happened to be among us riders on that trail ride?" Becky gingerly questioned, a smile sweeping across her lips as she thought back to that day two years ago.

"Oh, and of course, it was all helped by an angel, or some type of invisible helper, too. I'm sure you're going to say that next," Todd said, chuckling, while keeping his eyes forward on the road.

"Well, of course! Remember how we met, huh…huh?" Becky teased, gently poking the side of his shoulder.

"I'm sure I can't stop you from reminding me…again." Todd sighed, knowing she would continue which, she did.

"You surprised your friend Ron by coming out to Texas. He wasn't home. You found out he was going horseback riding. So, you came out to that ranch just as six of us were about ready to head out on the trail. Ron was so happy to see you. Suddenly, what happens, huh?" Becky jokingly questioned, just to rub it in a little.

"As soon as you walked toward us to talk to Ron," Becky's eyes widened, emphasizing her comment. "The young guy on the horse behind mine received a text. He had to dismount and leave. So, that horse was available. Just like that, you decided to take his place and ride with us. That's how we met. I rest my case." Becky and Todd both chuckled at her whimsical animations.

Todd pulled over to the side of the road and put the truck in park. He turned to her, drawing her close to his chest. He kissed her softly on the lips.

They were in love. He was going to surprise her by asking her to marry him later that night.

Becky tenderly gazed into Todd's eyes. "What was that kiss for?"

"Just because you're my girl," he said, brushing strands of hair away from her forehead.

"You just keep trying. Some day you just might convince me that what you say about an afterlife and invisible helpers is absolutely true."

"I'm gonna' make a total believer out of you yet, Todd Kramer," Becky said, a warm feeling rising within her. It felt so good to be with Todd.

"Listen," Todd said, "We're going to head back home. I'm taking you to a special place tonight, actually two places."

Todd told Becky he had booked reservations at her favorite restaurant, and after that, he was going to take her for an evening stroll along the parkway she really liked. Todd did not reveal his surprise proposal and engagement ring.

"My favorite restaurant? I'm hungry already!" Becky chimed happily and slid back to the passenger's side of the car, anticipating the upcoming evening events. She couldn't wait to enjoy the zucchini appetizer and wonderful grilled salmon salad, both specialty dishes that were pleasing to the palate and filling. Jack's Texas Grille didn't scrimp on portions either.

"Let's head back. Onward!" Becky playfully motioned.

"We're on our way!" With those words, Todd put the truck in drive, turned it around and headed back.

While driving on their way back, both were just listening to the tunes on the radio and enjoying the silent togetherness between them. Todd also took notice of the large semi-truck that had just turned onto the two-lane highway. It was coming toward them in the opposite lane.

"What's he doing?" Becky asked out loud. In the distance, she could also see the metallic, shiny rig begin to head towards the centerline of the highway.

Todd checked his speed and began to slow down.

"The driver probably just looked down for a second for some reason. I'm sure it will be okay," Todd said.

The driver did not slow the rig's speed.

Todd tried to reassure Becky, but it all happened so fast.

"Todd, watch out!" Becky's body stiffened when she saw what was happening and snapped the latch to her seat belt.

"I see it!" Todd gripped the wheel tightly, his eyes fixed on the fast-approaching big rig crossing into their lane.

"What's wrong with this driver?" Todd's apprehension was mounting fast. "Becky, he's…he is coming right at us!" Todd frantically warned.

The rig angled over the centerline heading right for them.

Todd quickly glanced the surroundings. If he jerked the wheel to the right, they would end up in a deep ditch with the car possibly rolling. He couldn't just slam on the brakes. Doing that could be as dangerous or worse for both of them should that big rig not stop. He also couldn't swerve left and chance hitting the rock bluff and flipping over.

He chose what he thought was the best.

"Todd, get your belt on!" Becky pleaded, as she softly began to cry.

"There's no time. Hold on!" Todd shouted, angry over what this man was doing.

He jerked the wheel to the right. He hoped he could maneuver somehow, brake hard, and force his vehicle to stop just before it went over into the ditch. He had to save his girl from harm.

Todd chose to swerve right. It was his only option.

"Chestnut, if there's ever a time for your beliefs to kick in, it's now!" Todd exclaimed, breathing hard and swerved toward the ditch hoping he could stop the truck in time.

The truck driver had also swerved to his right to get back over the centerline. The back of the rig was swaying back and forth like a long bulky snake, as it headed toward the berm on the rocky hillside of the road.

In one rapid and powerful moment, it was as if an invisible force separated them both at the last breath of a second, causing them to miss each other by inches.

"Did you see what happened? Did you feel that?" Todd exclaimed, as his pickup truck reached a screeching halt, just five feet from going over into the ditch.

Both vehicles were controlled without any harm to human life or the vehicles themselves. This invisible, yet almost palpable force stopped the rig from jackknifing or toppling onto its side. It also stopped Todd's pickup truck from careening into the deep ditch.

"Becky, are you alright?" Todd slid over and tenderly hugged her.

"Yes." Shaken, she whispered the word softly, wiping away tears of gratefulness that traced soft watery lines down her cheeks.

The mature, dark-haired, and partially bald rig driver jumped down out of the truck. He ran across the empty two-lane highway to quickly get to their vehicle.

"Are you both okay? I am so sorry. I don't know what the heck happened!" the truck driver said, breathing heavily.

"Again, I'm so sorry." The driver's shaken but apologetic tone was sincere as he leaned toward the open window on the driver's side of Todd's vehicle.

"The name's Pete," the rig driver said.

Dressed in black denim jeans and a cut-out sweatshirt that plainly exhibited his muscles, the rig driver showed relief. He stepped back as Todd and Becky both slid over to the driver's side to emerge from the pickup truck.

Todd was no longer angry. He was just as plainly shaken and confused as the truck driver was that nothing was damaged, and no one was hurt.

"Did you feel or see anything?" Todd asked, his amazement very apparent.

Todd looked at the husky rig driver dead in the eye and said, "I felt something. It was as if some invisible force came in between our trucks and instantly separated us. I cannot explain this, but sure as we're all standing here, I felt it!"

Todd turned toward Becky who stood quietly saying nothing. She knew this ordeal was his moment.

"We were all saved, I can tell you that!" Pete blurted out, as he brought his hand up and touched the gold, crucifix necklace he was wearing.

"What happened?" Todd asked.

"Man, I don't know." The uncertainty in Pete's voice was clearly evident.

"I was just driving and listening to the tunes on the radio. The windshield was clear. Then out of the blue, a large patch of dirt— or soot— I don't know. It just splattered the front window, totally blocking my view," Pete said, pointing back toward the windshield of his rig.

"I turned the wipers on as fast as I could. Next thing I know, my hands on the wheel felt like they were being pushed right. I swerved. I thought I couldn't control the rig, yet here we are, standing and able to talk about it." Pete exhaled, calming the adrenaline rush that welled up inside him.

"You actually felt something too?" Todd's mouth dropped open in surprise.

"Yes, I did! I can assure you of that. I never felt something like that before." Pete's emphatic sincerity was convincing.

The trucker turned to head back to the rig and motioned for Todd and Becky.

"Come see for yourselves, because I'm sure some of that dark stuff is still there on the windshield," Pete said, as Becky and Todd followed him across the empty highway.

Approaching the front of the semi-truck, they all looked up and saw a very dark, muddied type of film still visible. The wind shield wipers weren't very effective against this grimy attack that was spread across the window in a wide arch.

"I've traveled many a road." Pete placed his hands on hips. "And I can tell you without a doubt, this was a miracle. That's all I have to say about it."

Pete walked around to the passenger's side of the semi-truck, opened the door, and grabbed his wallet from inside the glove compartment. He came back around showing his driver's license to Todd in order to report the incident.

"No, Pete, that's not necessary. What counts is we're all okay."

Todd extended his hand toward the trucker.

"Well, I thank you very much for understanding," Pete said, shaking hands with Todd and giving Becky a quick smile.

"I didn't catch your name," Pete said.

"It's Todd."

"Thanks again." Pete turned and walked toward his truck.

The trucker climbed back up into his rig. He started the engine and windshield wipers to sweep away the rest of the film and slowly re-emerged on to the highway.

Becky and Todd held hands as they crossed back over the still-deserted highway and stood together behind his silver pickup.

"Becky, I'm..."

"You don't have to say anything to me, Todd. It's okay," Becky interrupted.

"But I want to say something." He touched her arm, stopping her to look at him. "I believe," he said, looking at her intently with sincere conviction.

"That was the Creator sending help, wasn't it?"

"Todd, in your heart, you knew it was," Becky said, breaking each other's gaze. She looked down and slid her shoe back and forth over some of the gravel.

"Well, the 'Man Upstairs' certainly got my attention! I must be a hard case," Todd said, cutting the last of the tension with humor while pulling her close to give her a big hug.

Later that night, Becky received yet another gift. Todd asked her to marry him.

> *"Faith is to believe what you do not see; the reward*
> *of this faith is to see what you believe."*
> —SAINT AUGUSTINE

TALE OF SISTER CHIPMUNK

BROTHER RABBIT HOPPED toward his nest, eager to get to safety. It was a quiet midmorning during spring in the Great Smoky Mountains National Park. Brother Rabbit felt the warmth of the sun on his light brown furry back as he scurried toward his nature den.

Approaching his little home just ahead of the forest's entrance of a large stand of birch, he was suddenly surprised by Sister Chipmunk, for he hadn't seen her in a long while. He shortened his gait and stopped beside her, sensing full well she was crying.

"What's wrong, Sister Chipmunk? You are so sad. You look as if you've lost a dear friend," Brother Rabbit said.

"I have," she sobbed as tears glided down the furry face and brown-striped body she was in the habit of so neatly primping over.

"You race like the roadrunners when you run across the field, and now I see you sitting here, a little lost lump of furry frowns. Can I help you in any way?" Brother Rabbit questioned, wanting to be of service.

"My heart feels heavy," Sister Chipmunk sighed, and pressed her back paws firmly on the soft green grass beneath her. She was exhausted and didn't want to lose balance.

The rabbit wanted to help her as much as possible, even though he knew he had to get back to his nest.

"What has happened to make your heart feel this way?" Brother Rabbit asked more firmly now, his black-buttoned nose wiggling distaste.

Brother Rabbit was very fond of his dear friend Sister Chipmunk. In fact, on a few occasions, he fleetingly thought that if she were of the same species, he would be her beau. However, as times and circumstances had willed it in their souls, this was not the lifetime for them. Yet his heart ached, now seeing her so sad.

"What happened?" He tried encouraging her to talk about what was bothering her.

"It happened to my friend, Fox," she replied through her whimpering.

Startled by her response, Brother Rabbit couldn't help but show how stunned he was. His breathing became visibly more rapid—his fur pulsing the rhythm of his breath. Then, hopping around in one small circle, shaken with distress, he finally settled next to her.

Brushing his paw against her tear-stained, furry face, the rabbit tried to comfort her.

"My gosh, Sister Chipmunk, you thought the fox was your friend?"

"Yes, I did. Even more than that, he wasn't typical. He really wasn't! I sensed it. He showed it. I know it to be an unlikely pair, but still our hearts were bound together. I trusted him. He took care of me," Sister Chipmunk said, dropping her head with a feeling of heavy sadness.

"How did he take care of you?" The rabbit asked somewhat suspiciously, for he knew the fox was their natural predator.

"Well, he made me laugh, believe it or not. He showed me his ways of the hunt, too. My friend, Fox told me the secrets of the fox's chase and told me how to avoid being hurt by another of his kind. Fox also helped me store my food for the winter."

Upon recalling, Sister Chipmunk felt a flicker of joy through her pain. It caused her to gingerly dart back and forth. Then just as quickly, she settled back again into a sitting position, her back paws firmly positioned within the green grass. She had to try and keep her balance.

"He let me nestle in his red-colored fur when I got cold, and we talked of many things," Sister Chipmunk said, but all the emotions seemed just too much for her tiny body. Her paws gave way. She fell sideways to the soft grassy earth, crying softly once again.

"Oh, please, stop crying. Everything will be all right," Brother Rabbit said and instinctively lifted her in his bulky paws, soothingly rocking her back and forth.

"An unlikely pair, indeed! Did you not sense or realize that the fox's normal instinct is to run and hide from larger predators, yet your species and mine are fair game to him? How could you have trusted him from the start?" Brother Rabbit questioned, trying to make sense of all of this.

"Sister Chipmunk, I know it hurts to talk about it, but please speak to me so that I may understand your reasoning."

"I didn't trust him at the beginning, but as time went on, he showed me the real meaning of trust," Sister Chipmunk said, darting away from the rabbit's gentle hold.

"Let me show you what he taught me."

The chipmunk picked up a tiny stick with her furry paw and

made a clean, soft canvas of dirt with which to write in a language, of course, that is used and understood by only the animals in the forest.

Slowly, painfully, Sister Chipmunk wrote these words for Brother Rabbit to see.

"This is what Fox spelled out," she said and then showed him:

T—To

R—Realize that

U—Under God every

S—Species should be

T—Treated with respect.

He was so surprised that he held his own breath for that moment of such a great and important realization. Even though it was not that way now in the forest or anywhere, Brother Rabbit understood what the fox meant. It struck a powerful chord within his own small, beating heart.

"Where is your friend the fox? What has happened?"

Sister Chipmunk dropped the small stick and slowly lifted her head. She looked straight into Brother Rabbit's brown eyes and began talking.

"It was one of his own kind, wanting to snatch…me…away." Sister Chipmunk spoke slowly at first.

"We were in our favorite field. This…this… intruder pushed his way in. It was horrible. Fox fought with his own kind for me. They struggled, snarled… tore at each other!" Sister Chipmunk furrowed her little brow, her front paw swiping at some blades of grass.

"The intruder was not acting like himself; something was very wrong. Then I saw my friend's look." Sister Chipmunk sighed heavily, not sure whether to continue.

"What look?" Brother Rabbit urged her to keep going.

"It was his glance. My friend Fox was ready to give his life for me. I saw it in his pain-filled amber eyes when he looked over at me. Fox tried to push me away, told me to run, but I couldn't move. I felt frozen, as I helplessly watched what was happening." The anguish sound in her chip-chip chatter echoed softly through the trees nearby.

"Then, the cracking of fallen branches breaking under pressure scared that wild-eyed fox intruder." Sister Chipmunk was crying hard again.

"Oh, Sister Chipmunk…" was all Brother Rabbit could force out of his own throat, for he was crying too.

"I couldn't run. I didn't want to," Sister Chipmunk said, blurting out the words. "Then something happened, and everything just went dark in front of my eyes." She paused, twitching her contrasting dark and light-brown striped tail nervously.

"I must have fainted, because the next thing I saw when I woke up was my friend Fox, lying on the ground near me. I could hear the faint sound of his breathing. The other fox had run away."

"You don't have to tell me more," Brother Rabbit pleaded.

Sister Chipmunk continued anyway. "He struggled, slowly stretching his paw for the stick…" her voice trailed off.

"Sister Chipmunk, are you okay?" Brother Rabbit asked, not sure if she could continue or even if he wanted her to keep talking.

She looked up at Brother Rabbit and said, "My friend Fox, he… he slowly spelled out another word before he died. It…it was the word, 'Love.'"

"I love you the more in that I believe you had liked
me for my own sake and for nothing else."
—JOHN KEATS

THE PRAYER BUNDLE

"IT'S NOT FAIR! Johnny Running Deer's father told me that if I put up these prayer bundles and talked, You would listen to me! Haven't You heard me?" The sixteen-year-old young man yelled up at the sky to God, the Creator, as tears of frustration rolled down his cheeks. Danny's dog was lost and still had not been found.

Angrily swiping a fallen tear away from his cheek, Danny stooped down turning his lean, athletic form toward the creek. The blue denim shirt and jeans he wore were his comfortable attire when out in the woods.

Tired from the emotional frustration, Danny leaned over and picked up a couple of small round stones. Straightening back up, he paused for a moment, threw them hard, and watched them skip across the water. Nature pleased him much more than staying inside and being on the computer or playing video games.

Danny had experienced various types of outdoor adventures with his three-year-old border-collie mix. As animals go, this dog was Danny's best buddy. He was really taken with her and her coloring. She was all white and had unusual, beautiful black spots and patches scattered over her body. He also marveled that one-half of her face was black and the other half was white—the colors were split perfectly even on both sides of her face. His dog was well-muscled and athletic.

He thought that the dog's markings looked like a Pinto horse, so he named her Pinto.

Wanting to please her young master, Pinto was a good dog and listened really well. The two of them enjoyed each other's company and understood each other in each of their own ways. They were almost inseparable.

Danny's father, an ex-Navy veteran and survivalist, taught his son some of the ways of tracking in the woods. So, two weeks after Danny was shown the true basics of tracking, he decided to give Pinto her first lesson. That's when he lost her.

"I shouldn't have done it out in the woods like that. Dad warned me not to try and train her without boundaries for her first time. I should have listened." Danny spoke the words out loud, as he tossed another stone hard across the water. He could hear the loud "plunk" of that small rock echo along the dirt walls of the creek bed as it hit the water then sank.

The autumn season was one of Danny's favorite times of the year. Just fourteen days ago, he and his dog Pinto were both running and trekking in the woods. For protection, Danny's dad made sure his son carried a strong pepper spray while in the woods not too far from the house.

The house Danny Carver lived in sat on a small hill, with the back of it overlooking about nine acres of wooded property. Some of that back property belonged to Danny's family, some of it didn't. A distance away to be sure, but he still didn't think it was too far from Slaty Fork, West Virginia. Living where he did was like being in city and country combined.

Danny's mom and dad did not allow him to go too far past a

tree-lined boundary they set. There were times he would sneak a little farther into the wooded area anyway. Danny and Pinto evaded that boundary limit once again just two weeks ago.

"I shouldn't have tried to teach her. I've lost her," he muttered to himself, his head bowed toward the ground.

Danny recalled that everything was going well with Pinto's lesson until the unexpected and frightening surprise occurred. Danny and Pinto suddenly came face to face with a large, angry, and intimidating male coyote.

This coyote had been silently stalking them, measuring whether it could target the dog as prey.

Both Danny and Pinto stopped short in their tracks, stiffening against a potential attack. "Steady girl, stay," he softly murmured the words to his companion animal.

Hackles rising across her entire back, Pinto stood still, growling. Her coffee-colored eyes locked onto the large, dark-haired male predator. For a few moments, the coyote and border- collie mix stood as if frozen in time—invisible clashing energy mounting.

His own adrenaline rising, Danny could now feel the fight or flight sensation build up momentum inside him—inside them, too. "Stay Pinto!" Danny commanded.

"Coyotes usually don't act this way because Pinto's not a small dog and I'm with her.

Something's wrong!" His thoughts raced as he tried to gauge the situation.

The coyote wasn't close enough for Danny to use the strong pepper spray. He didn't have a large, thick walking stick in his hands either, something his dad would constantly remind him to carry.

Danny couldn't think fast enough at first, but one thing was for sure. He wasn't going to let that coyote harm his dog.

Pinto sensed Danny's feelings. That's when his dog decided for him. She was his protector.

Barking and snapping, the dog lunged forward.

"Pinto! Pinto!" Danny screamed out her name trying to stop her from chasing the coyote. It didn't help. He could see she showed no fear and was dead set on chasing and fighting with this coyote if she had to.

The coyote, stunned at the dog's show of courage and real threat, suddenly backed down, spun away from her, and ran. Pinto now became coyote's predator.

"Pinto, come back! Come here!" Danny saw how fast she was going, chasing right behind the coyote. He also knew that if pushed to the limit, this coyote would turn on his dog and could kill her.

His desperate calls were to no avail. Both were faster than he was. Danny stopped running, breathing hard. Panic began to set in as he saw them disappear from his sight.

"Please Creator, don't let my dog get hurt! What if she runs into a pack of them?" Danny turned and ran as fast as he could back to the house to get his dad. He knew his mom, who worked for a rescue animal group, would be worried and upset, too.

Danny sat down on the dirt near the creek. Having recalled that awful experience just two weeks ago, he rested his arms on his knees and tried to relax.

"It's my fault!" Danny exclaimed. "I shouldn't have taken her out like that…I…I just shouldn't have." He buried his head in his arms feeling the tears slide down his cheeks.

Danny heard the sound of crackling leaves. He quickly wiped the tears from his eyes, lifted his head and turned toward that sound.

"Hey!" Johnny Running Deer called out in a lighthearted voice, as he jumped down from the small incline, landing upright on both feet. Johnny knew how bad off Danny was emotionally.

These two best friends were so different. Danny had shorter and wavy, honey-colored hair. His eyes were aquamarine blue. Johnny, on the other hand, had shoulder length thick and smooth dark hair that he often wore in a ponytail positioned at the base of his neck. Johnny was lean and well-muscled. He was six feet tall, four inches taller than his best friend. Danny was white-skinned but tanned in the summer, which was the only time he looked a bit closer to Johnny's light, copper-colored skin tone.

Johnny Running Deer's father would often remark that even though they were different, they are brothers in spirit and in their hearts. They walked in a good way together. Both Danny and Johnny were about four years apart in age. Johnny, twenty years of age, was the older one. Both learned from each other, laughed with each other, and were loyal friends. They both would get mad at each other, too, when one of them got just as stubborn as the other.

Danny thought he was getting the better end of the deal concerning this friendship. He could see how, in such a good and harmonious way, Johnny respected nature and all life and shared some of the knowledge and ways of his Lakota Native American heritage with Danny. "Creator made it," Johnny Running Deer would often say, pointing to that bush, tree, or that animal.

"Your prayers will be heard. I know it!" Johnny said, walking over and placing his hand on Danny's shoulder.

"They haven't been so far," Danny responded with a rough edge of agitation.

He rose sharply to his feet and kicked the dirt in front of him. "Why can't we find her?" Danny asked.

"You want it on your time, that's why, and you won't let go enough to trust the Creator to work on this problem." Johnny spoke the words calmly hoping Danny's emotions would settle.

"Well, I can't wait. I waited long enough. If God is too busy, I'll handle it on my own!" Danny snapped back with an angry, narrowed look.

To Johnny, his best friend's reactions were okay, because Danny was hurting and was just releasing emotions. Yet Johnny knew through experience that impatience and angry frustration could lead to a lesson. He could see the signs that it was coming.

"Come on now, give your prayers more of a chance. Be more patient. You'll see. The Creator hears you!" Johnny said, emphatically making his point, by raising the index finger of his right hand up to the sky.

"I don't mean any disrespect," Danny said, having placed his right hand firmly on his hip, "but I don't think the Creator has enough time for me, and I don't have enough patience for Him at the moment. The longer He waits, the worse it is for me not to have my dog back! I'm scared she's hurt really bad—or dead!"

Danny was visibly shaken, totally frustrated, and feeling guilty. All of it he could feel balled up into a knot in his stomach.

"I'll talk to you later. I'm going to handle this now on my own!" Storming past Johnny, he decided to stop, standing with his back toward his friend.

"You're my friend and my brother, Johnny. Thanks for being here, but I just can't wait anymore!" With those spoken words, Danny rushed to climb the small incline and head up the hill.

The lesson came—quicker than lightning and as swift as a sudden breeze. Surefooted Danny slipped halfway up just past the incline and rolled back down, bouncing back on to the dirt of the creek bed. He wasn't hurt, but found himself stretched out on his stomach, his face in the dirt near where Johnny was standing.

"You're not going anywhere my friend—at least not at the

moment!" Johnny chuckled, as he looked down at the back of Danny's wavy-haired head.

Danny looked up at Johnny. "I can't believe it! I've never missed a step going up that incline." Danny was annoyed as he got to his feet, dusting himself off.

"Here," Johnny said, pulling something out of the pocket of his black jeans. "I wanted you to have this. I was supposed to give you this before you stormed off. With what just happened, I know now you were definitely meant to have it."

Johnny gave him a small vinyl-covered card. On the front was a beautiful sunset scene with trees. On the back was a poem:

LET GO AND LET GOD

As children bring their broken toys
With tears for us to mend,
I brought my broken dreams to God,
Because He was my friend.
But then, instead of leaving Him
In peace, to work alone,
I hung around and tried to help
With ways that were my own.
At last, I snatched them back and cried,
"How can You be so slow?"
"My child," He said,
"What could I do?
You never did let go."

(Lauretta P. Burns—1957)

Danny wasn't in the mood at all, but he looked at the picture side anyway, thought about it for a second, then flipped the card over.

He read it.

Holding the card in one hand, and brushing his hair back with the other, Danny just kept staring, focusing on that last line. He didn't even notice his friend left.

No one was there except himself and the soft sounds of the moving creek water. He also knew Johnny left on purpose to let him think about things on his own.

"Wow!" was all Danny could whisper. Between the card he read and the fall he took, he got the lesson really quick. He needed his own reminder to be more patient and to trust.

"I'm sorry I got mad and wasn't patient," Danny called out, looking up toward the sky. "It's just hard for me. I'm scared my dog got chewed up and died a horrible death because of me!"

Finally, those guilt-ridden words spewed from his mouth. Danny felt better after he said them and heard the words echo away over the creek's calming waters.

"Okay, I'll wait. I'll let You handle it. But make it soon," Danny said. "Please!"

A few days later Danny came back to the creek. It was a special and serene place for him to be. He was sitting on a tree stump, brushing off his jeans from a few of the wet, autumn leaves that had stuck to his pant leg. That's when he caught a side glance of an animal racing toward him. That's also when he heard the barking. His heart leapt. It was Pinto.

"Pinto, I missed you so much!" Danny stooped down to greet the barking happy pet that ran toward his open arms.

Danny hugged her and hugged her. When he released his hold, Pinto would run around him, wagging her tail and rush back into his arms again. This went on for a while, until they both calmed down.

"Told you," Johnny said with a beaming smile, knowing the Creator would come through. Danny knew Johnny had a habit of just showing up—out of nowhere—and always at the right times.

"I'm glad she's back!" Johnny added. "Your dad wanted me to bring her here to you. He's back up at the house, beaming a wide grin from ear to ear." Johnny Running Deer bent over to pat Pinto on the head. "She is healthy too, see?"

"Yeah, I can see, and I'm so glad!" Danny said, then called his dog to start back to the house with them.

"How did she get back? What happened?" Danny could hardly contain himself he was so excited—so urgent with the questioning as he walked alongside his friend.

"Nothing is impossible for the Creator. You got that now?" Johnny asked and smiling, he ruffled up the hair on Danny's head.

"Yeah, yeah, I got it…I got it. But, how?" Danny pressed the question while smoothing his hair back down.

"Well, Pinto chased off the coyote alright. She ran that male away for a good long while, but she got herself tangled in some brush somehow. That brush was pretty thick, too. Pinto was stuck and hidden from the open path."

"I'm so glad you're okay," Danny said, stopping abruptly and stooped down to hug Pinto again. The dog responded with happy whimpering and a rapid wagging of her tail. It acted like wind that brushed away some leaves laying on the ground.

"Uh, where did you go?" Johnny asked, looking to his side not realizing his friend had stopped and was petting Pinto.

"Are you starting to learn to do what I do—that 'now you see me, now you don't' kind of stuff? Johnny laughed, as he turned back to see the both of them—two-legged human and four-legged animal—enjoying their reunion.

Danny jogged his way to catch up. Pinto was right behind. The soft, crackling sound of the yellow-gold and orange foliage under his feet was a sound that warmed his heart. Danny felt a sense of peace wash over him.

"Sorry for the distraction. I'm just happy Pinto wasn't hurt really bad or killed," Danny said.

"Okay," Johnny said, patting Danny on the back and continued.

"The lady jogger who found her said the dog was lucky she did, but she couldn't find any tags. Pinto had been stuck in that brush for maybe more than a couple of days. It was good the dog had run-off creek water to drink." Johnny eyed the dog and continued. "Your dog had scratches and a cut on the back leg with a pulled muscle. The lady coaxed your limping pet to her car and drove Pinto to the vet. That is where she has been until now." Johnny fell silent and waited for his friend to respond.

"How, then, was my dog able to come home?" Danny questioned.

"Your dad said it was like a miracle. He felt led somehow, to be in the right place at the right time, and there she was. Anyway, your dad will give you the details," Johnny said, putting a hand on Danny's shoulder.

"You know, it has been a good day—for all of us," Johnny acknowledged and was grateful for it.

Late that night, Danny quietly snuck outside the back door and looked up at the clear, starlit night sky.

"Thank you," Danny said, and walked over to tie another prayer bundle onto a low-lying branch of the tulip tree.

"This is a gift for you, Creator, and I just want to say that I learned the lesson."

With that said, Danny turned around and headed back to the house. It was a very good day for sure. It was a good night, too.

"We long for affection altogether ignorant of our faults. Heaven has accorded this to us in the uncritical canine attachment"
—George Eliot

Two-Way Trail

"I CAN'T BELIEVE she's gone!"

Shania was alone in the small, empty log cabin catching the faint, comforting aroma of sage. This rustic lodge was her soul-centering and peaceful home away from home—off the beaten path in the Blue Ridge Mountain area of North Carolina.

The thirty–year old, tall, and slim-shaped woman sat down on the multi-colored blanketed bed. She ran her slender, copper-colored fingers through her short dark hair, feeling totally stunned by the emptiness of the cabin.

It took some minutes before she could get up and walk over to the black walnut rocker. The soft sounds of her own bootsteps echoed the emptiness. The sting of her mentor's sudden departure had caught her off guard.

"My teacher, and my friend," Shania said, tears welling up and flowing down her cheeks like tiny streams.

She stood behind the rocker, which was her teacher's favorite piece of furniture. Clutching its top with both hands, Shania remembered all the times she sat at the feet of her mentor who would rock back and forth while sharing teachings and stories.

Just two years ago, on that warm autumn morning, Shania had been very upset. She was sitting near a stream off the side of the wooded-trail path.

"Why is it that I seem to be the one who does most of the contacting to keep in touch with people I care about? When I mention I haven't heard from them, the answer is always the same. They are just too busy!" Shania, exclaiming it all out loud, seemed as if she was speaking directly to the softly rushing river.

"You know," she said, continuing to talk to that river of water, "I've about had enough! It's getting tiring."

Shania was distracted by having noticed a small turtle shuffling toward the water. She nudged it gently into the river and watched it skillfully swim away alongside the edge of the watery bank.

Feelings of aggravation bristled through her like a scouring sponge. At that same moment she heard a soft rustling of the gold and orange autumn leaves breaking the sound of silence along the trail.

"Who's there?"

Shania felt her heart quicken its beat. She turned her head toward the sound and saw someone approaching her.

The image was of a hardy small-framed mature woman. With long, thick salt and pepper gray hair, Shania could see that part of it had been pulled back and fastened somehow; the rest of this woman's hair lay low to her shoulders in a messy, yet complimentary way.

"The sounds within the river told me you were here and wanted me to come," this mysterious and spunky mature woman said, as she casually sat down near Shania.

"By the way, my name's Wind. What's yours?" she asked, looking at Shania with a penetrating, yet comforting ocean-blue gaze.

Shania noticed the woman's attire. It was, in its way, especially unique, although simple— pants, top and boots. The pants and top were made of genuine brown deer skin. The woman's western, boot-style shoes matched the color of the rest of her garment. Around the woman's neck were a gold cross and a beautiful turquoise swash blossom. The size of both necklaces fit in perfect balance to Wind's entire frame.

"My name is Shania, and the sounds of the water told you I was here?" Shania couldn't believe it. For a moment, she felt nervous wondering if this woman was off her rocker or something.

"I heard those thoughts, and no I'm not off my rocker, but I do have a rocking chair in my log cabin that I really like."

Wind smiled sheepishly, knowing what she just said might unnerve Shania, but Wind also knew this young woman wouldn't run away.

"Okay, sensing my thoughts and talking about them has me rattled. I don't know who you are and why you suddenly showed up, but now you really are making me nervous!"

Shania slid a little farther away from Wind, quietly deciding whether to get up and leave or stay put.

"I told you. I showed up because the sounds of the river told me, and here I am. Oh, and don't be nervous. It doesn't help the digestion. You're already upset enough!"

Wind gave Shania a side-wink and smiled which she could see relieved this woman's edginess.

"You want to come over for lunch?" Wind asked and waited for the response.

"I've got to tell you, I'm hesitant, but I will," Shania said, surprised with her own response while brushing off some autumn leaves that had fallen on her pale gray sweatshirt and blue jeans.

Something about this woman made her feel as if she had known Wind for a long while, yet they only just now met. Her own edginess began to fade.

Shania began to feel a pleasant and invisible wave of connection with Wind. It was something she couldn't explain—at least not at this moment.

"Well okay then, off we go," Wind said, extending her hand for Shania to grasp.

They stood up together with Wind leading the way back to her vintage green pickup truck.

That was the start of Shania West's two-year training under Wind's tutelage regarding nature's ways and God's ways. Shania learned more of how to be in the world and yet not of it. Their connection also blossomed into a significant friendship both had with one another.

However, there were times Wind would say, "There would come a day when…", but stopped short of saying what that meant or anything more. Nor would Wind ever explain it, no matter how hard Shania would press the issue.

Now, two years later, Wind's personally treasured and natural-made items scattered along the log cabin shelves were gone. Her especially favored leather-bound book was also missing. It was the one book Shania often found Wind reading and reflecting upon.

The small wooden picnic table that usually held her tea kettle, coffee, and fresh fruits, along with walnuts and fresh-baked banana bread was bare. The bench itself was gone.

Recently lit cabin fires had turned to gray ash lying on the fireplace floor. The sound of Wind's little squirrel friends scurrying back and forth had vanished into thin air.

The sound of silence was deafening. A chilly and empty feeling came over Shania. The only small comfort she had was that faint aroma of cleansing sage.

The emotional trigger came fast, struck hard, then side-railed off its pathway when Shania saw the folded ivory-colored paper lying on the rocking chair seat.

"I was just here last weekend! What is going on?" Shania murmured her surprise yet knowing full well her teacher was gone and would not be returning.

She leaned over and picked up the ivory paper then walked around to the front of the rocker, so she could sit down in it.

"It feels so good sitting here, Wind. It's like being able to still feel your presence."

Shania's softly spoken words trailed off, as one teardrop fell from her cheek and moistened the folded note.

"Okay, I'll read what you wanted to say," Shania whispered, opening the folded paper.

"Now, you know I don't always talk in full sentences, and you know I like to get to the point. So here it is," began the words on the page. Shania smiled remembering her teacher's unique ways of communicating at times.

"I hope that sting of loneliness came quickly and went," Wind had written.

"She knew I'd feel this way," Shania quietly acknowledged and continued to read.

"I don't like good-byes; don't believe in them because we're never really gone from each other anyway. Just remember," Wind wrote, "Don't believe that anyone is too busy all the time. There's a give and take in life and relationships, and it's for darn good reasons. Remember the balance!"

Shania smiled softly, as another tiny tear slid off her lower dark lashes and glided quickly toward her cheek. She remembered the many different ways Wind had to keep repeating that lesson, so Shania would truly understand.

"You and I had a give and take in ways you may not even real-ize." Shania was so surprised Wind had written this because Shania always thought Wind had given so much more to her.

Shania wanted to giggle and outright cry at the same time. She didn't know which to do first, because the memories of their time shared were so endearing and everlasting.

Wiping some tears away, she looked back down at the note.

"Dang, oops! Sorry about that—had to pause a minute. That one pesky, keep-coming-back squirrel ran in and jumped on the table again to grab some of the walnuts!" Shania noticed the writing had scrambled a bit, as if Wind's hand had been pushed.

"That little imp caused me to jump! I almost had to write this all over again. You think I'd learn to know better already and not get rattled. Think the little imp does it on purpose!"

Shania giggled a bit more now than she cried for the missing of her friend.

"Anyway," the writing continued. "You now know—really know—what a two-way trail means, when it's necessary to have and what to do if you find you don't have that balance. I gave you the sign to know these things in case you don't remember."

Wind's writing broke off. Shania could tell by the way the words ended abruptly. Then she saw a tiny paw print on the page and laughed out loud.

"Shoot, that pesky but lovable friend did it again! Well, now you've got the stamped approval of this note—squirrel paw print!"

Shania stopped reading for a moment and laid her head back. She closed her eyes and started gently rocking back and forth, remembering.

What flooded her thoughts was the memory of the squirrel running in and sitting atop the table closely observing what Wind was doing. Then it would snatch a walnut, find the escape path, and run. It was this squirrel's regular routine.

Shania remembered it was even more humorous to watch Wind's show of playful and affectionate reactions to the squirrel's friendly responses of purring and frisky mischief.

After those few moments, she came back to the present, looked down and continued reading.

"If you fall back into that one-sided energy, just remember the sign—my rockin' chair! Oh heck, take it with you. Sit in it and let it sway you back and forth in a good and balanced way. You'll remember."

Shania's heart leapt, realizing she was taking home with her a special part of Wind's life—her rocking chair.

There were so many wonderful as well as challenging experiences she had gone through due to Wind's teaching and friendship, that there came bubbling up from within her, a sense of peace and joy. It washed over her entire being. She didn't want the words Wind wrote to end, but knew, of course, they would.

Looking back down at that ivory-colored paper, the student read the final words her mentor had written.

"The wind blows where it wishes, and you hear its sound, but you do not know where it comes from or where it goes. So it is with everyone who is born of the Spirit."—John 3:8. Yep, it comes from Scripture. So, that's also good to know and remember, Shania."

"Well, time for me to go," Wind wrote. "The Spirit willing, we'll meet again—someday, somewhere, whether here in this natural world or in the heavens above. I carry you in my heart—always! Wind."

Within that empty log cabin came the instant feeling of a gentle breeze blowing. How it happened, Shania no longer questioned, for she experienced many unusual things in the company of her teacher. It just proved once again that her mentor was the real deal—authentic.

She folded the note back up, placed it on her lap and quietly rested. Shania stayed there for a long while, rocking back and forth in that walnut-made comfort.

Suddenly, she was jerked from her peaceful state. The very man she cared for, but with whom she usually had to make the first contact, rushed into the cabin.

"Shania, I haven't heard from you at all! I tried texting and calling you. No answer. Then I remembered where you once told me you would go at times, and I came searching for you."

Nathan's words and actions were obviously sincere as he approached Shania. This tall, well-muscled and brown-eyed man had been worried.

Regardless of her surprise, the only thought Shania had when she looked up at him was, "It's time now for me to practice what I've learned."

> *"Happiness is not a matter of intensity but of*
> *balance, order, rhythm and harmony."*
> —THOMAS MERTON

Acknowledgments

Before this full work was just a wisp of an idea, some initial advocates—you know who you are—gave "thumbs up" for me to bring the idea into form. Thank you, Debbi, Anne, and Claire, who offered initial assistance.

This is a personal message to you Paul; you've traveled the up and down roads with me. You have been a loyal supporter of my work. A meaningful hug and thanks go to you.

Jane, your artwork visually brought scenes and characters to life within these written pages.

Jill Sell, poet and journalist in her own right was there to offer me some tips.

Corinne O'Connor, your support in various ways unfolded at the times I needed most. Colleen, you added a watchful gaze by checking for the little things that could easily be missed in a manuscript.

A *Special Thanks* goes to you, Lori Kalina, who gave primary support. Your loyalty, enthusiasm, and the care you provided has been such a valuable contribution to this book and to me.

I also wish to thank you, George Novotney, Jr. for your legal insight, timeless connection, and humor.

Above all, thank you Lord our Creator. Words cannot express the gratitude I feel. Yet, I'm not worried if I can't verbally express them. You already know what my words would be. Knowing that truth, I am content.

About the Author and Illustrator

Author: Karen David currently resides on the outskirts of Cleveland, Ohio in a fairytale-like bungalow nestled on three acres of land amid tall trees and wildlife where she has also owned and boarded horses.

Karen, who is an Intuitive and a woman of faith, has walked along a road less journeyed. She also has sponsored classes, workshops, and has traveled extensively in addition to her private consulting practice. Her desire to serve stems from her own Catholic faith and having learned about other religious and spiritual practices, including some Native American understanding which was shared with her.

She gained the understanding of discernment in addition to the wisdom needed in regard to trusting her own unique intuition.

Karen also feels that this particular book was an inspired gift; these storytelling tales of transformation and hope…stepping stones toward inner awareness and healing.

Illustrator: Jane Sibley-Hager completed a Bachelor of Art and Art History at McMaster University in Hamilton, Ontario Canada. She was also fortunate in having had a career teaching high school art which she loved. Her students had helped her to grow as a person, an artist, and a teacher. She continues to explore ways to use art as a medium for communication and growth. **Jane** was given her first opportunity by Karen, the Author, to express her artistry seen in this book; this type of artistry had never been done before by her. She currently lives in North Carolina with her husband, seven cats and two dogs.

www.ingramcontent.com/pod-product-compliance
Lightning Source LLC
Chambersburg PA
CBHW021000160726
47994CB00006B/2318